TINK AND THE LOST BOYS

BY

T.J. SPADE
&
MONTANA ASH

Published by Paladin Publishing

Tink And The Lost Boys
Copyright © 2019 by Montana Ash & T.J. Spade

All rights reserved

This is a work of fiction. Names, characters, businesses, places, events, and incidents are either the products of the author's imagination or used in a fictitious manner. Any resemblance to actual persons, living or dead, or actual events is purely coincidental.

This book or any portion thereof may not be reproduced or used in any manner whatsoever without the express written permission of Montana Ash and T.J. Spade, except for the use of brief quotations embodied in critical articles and reviews.

Cover design by: Take Cover Designs
Formatting by: LKO Designs
ISBN: 9781072982913

To Laura,
Enjoy Tink + her guys!
Montana Ash.

A NOTE FROM THE AUTHORS

As authors (and readers) we both like our relationships to be fully inclusive. This means there are sexy-times between all characters – including the men (m/m). So, please note that Tink And The Lost Boys contains sexually explicit material between three men and one woman in a reverse harem/polyamorous relationship and is only intended for adults.

T.J. & Montana xoxo

CHAPTER ONE

Tink gritted her teeth and cast her eyes toward the ceiling, silently asking the Powers That Be for patience. *Lots* of patience. Pan – friend, confidant, and president of their little motorcycle club – had just walked into the kitchen wearing nothing but loose-fitting grey sleep-pants and an adorable grumpy frown as he headed to the coffee maker. The machine was a state-of-the-art masterpiece, large and shiny, perched in pride of place in the centre of the large kitchen island. It dutifully fulfilled its purpose numerous times a day by providing the nectar of the Gods so the entire household could function. Tink had already had her first cup and had been attempting to make her escape before Pan inevitably moseyed into the kitchen in all his sinfully sexy, sleep-tousled glory like he did every morning. The man was completely oblivious to the way his light brown hair fell rakishly over his blue eyes, or the way his right hand scratched absently at his washboard abs as he yawned and stretched, arching his back and affording her the perfect view of his muscled arse.

Tink barely refrained from whimpering. The man's butt was what dreams were made of. She shifted in her seat, willing her wings to behave as they began to flutter against her back. They may have been pretty but they often had a mind of their own, their frenetic movements a direct reflection of her thoughts and feelings. They also had a nasty habit of sprinkling fairy dust when she was turned-on. Which, in the presence of her esteemed leader, was; All. The. Time. Thankfully, in all his male ignorance, Pan remained completely oblivious to the cause of her technicoloured glitter. Instead, he believed she lacked control over the appendages, and thus, also her innate magical abilities. In reality, that couldn't be farther from the truth. Tink was a fairy – one of the last pure-blood fairies in existence. And as such, she was one of the only beings on the planet who could make pure magic. Even in their largely mortal and human-dominated society, there were still hundreds of supernatural beings living in secret who could manipulate and use magic. But no species other than the fairies were born with the ability to create it. The result of being so 'special'? Tink was highly sought after by friend and foe alike. She was as dangerous as she was miraculous, and when fairy numbers – and therefore, magic – began to dwindle in the world, extreme measures were put into place to ensure they didn't become extinct.

Tink snorted, cracking a grin, though it held no humour. The control measures were nothing but shackles to her freedom. She loathed the laws and regulations set down by the Magical

Committee and had been finding loopholes to buck their system since she was a teenager. She knew her luck would soon run out and she would need to submit to their archaic and unreasonable stipulations. In fact, her mind was taken up with such thoughts on a daily basis and she was yet to think of a workable solution. Her family – The Lost Boys MC – could only shelter and protect her for so long. Tink wasn't stupid, she knew Pan received *offers* for her all the time. She also knew he turned down every single one. But one day, an offer, or rather a threat, would be made that he couldn't refuse. Or her thirty-second birthday would lapse – whichever came first – and then where would she be? Bound to a consort she loathed, wings tethered and useless, doomed to be nothing more than a magical blood bag and brood mare.

"Something funny?"

Tink's morose thoughts came to a grinding halt as her best friend spoke, obviously referring to Tink's sarcastically amused chuckle moments before. Wendy was one of only three humans in their club, with her brothers – Jon and Michael – being the other two. The three humans had stumbled upon the best kept secret of the world – magic – by accident. As an eighteen-year-old, Jon had been drawn to Caden, the oldest member of the MC. Even ten years ago, Caden had been a silver fox. Big and muscly, dark hair streaked with greys, neatly trimmed beard even more liberally sprinkled with the silver strands, Caden had been exactly what Jon had wanted. And what Jon wanted, Jon got. Tink smiled genuinely this time, marvelling at the strength and will of humans. Jon had somehow achieved the impossible; monogamy. He had been in an exclusive relationship with Caden for ten years, effectively becoming a part of the family and the already-established motorcycle club. Why was it so impressive that Jon and Caden had been in an exclusive and dedicated relationship for so long? Because Caden was a nymph. A male nymph. Just like the other six male members of the club – including Pan. Oh yeah, that's right; nymphs.

Tink was surrounded by seven highly sexual, hugely sensual, male nymphs on a daily basis. Not only were they flawless specimens of nature, from their shiny hair, to their perfectly chiselled cheekbones, and proportionately muscled frames. They also exuded sex and lust from their pores like sweat. Magical beings and humans alike were helpless against their charms, multitudes of males and females fell at their feet, wanting nothing more than to pleasure – and be pleasured – by the perfectly beautiful nymphs. Tink couldn't blame them. She wanted the exact same thing. At least, she wanted it from Pan – the object of her unrequited lust and something more. The something more she was still in full denial mode about because the feelings were useless. Pan was a nymph. He was *the* male nymph – what amounted to the king of their kind. There was no way he would, or even could, settle for one sexual partner like Caden had managed to do. Not only was it against their unwritten rules, but it was also against their nature. Tink understood the nymph's need for flirting and sex. They fed off the sexual energies of others – it sustained them. If they didn't get enough sex or expose themselves to enough lust, they became ill and could even die. So, she understood. Really, she did. But it didn't make her feelings any easier to deal with.

Eyeing Pan one last time, Tink sighed, her breath ruffling her white-blonde hair, "No. Nothing is funny," she answered Wendy.

Wendy gave her a sympathetic look, patting her on her arm. Being her best friend and the only other female member of the club, Wendy of course knew all about Tink's useless affections. Wendy kept her secret like any good soul-sister would, but that didn't mean she kept her opinions to herself. The pretty strawberry-blonde was under the misguided belief that Tink should come clean with her feelings. *All* of her feelings. Including the matching ones she had for Pan's two lieutenants. That's right, she was a glutton for punishment. Not only was she in lust/love with Pan, she also had the exact same warm, fuzzy feelings for Nate and Tao. The three were practically inseparable – best friends and no doubt, lovers – for dozens of years. She wasn't naïve; she knew they shared sexual conquests. Nymphs were the most equal-opportunity beings you could come across. They didn't distinguish between gender, race, or religion. They didn't care about size, or weight, or hair colour. No, nymphs didn't use their eyes to see beauty or judge attraction. They were instead drawn to a person's lust. The more lustful or sexual an individual's appetite, the more attractive you were to a nymph. And what sharpened lust? Multiple bodies writhing around in pleasure in a confined space.

Tink's wings trembled again, a direct reflection of her

excitement from picturing Pan, Nate, and Tao naked and writhing on a bed with *her* in the centre instead of some random hook up. She clenched her fists, anger and jealousy quickly replacing her fantasy. She understood the inherent nature of nymphs, she really did. And she didn't blame the boys for what they needed to do to survive. But that didn't mean she had to like it. It was why she stayed well away from a certain floor at the club they owned. She had witnessed more than her fair share of her nymphs with other people. When it had started to cause a physical ache in the region of her heart, she couldn't pinpoint exactly, but subtly and slowly over time, her feelings had changed. Now she was in the almost laughable predicament of being in love with three male nymphs. The other two of which, chose that moment to enter the kitchen looking all sexily sleep rumpled.

Likely because they had been having sex all night long! Tink muttered bitchily inside her head. The residents of their club house got more arse than a toilet seat, while she abstained from all acts of sex in silent, torturous protest. And on that lovely note, Tink took a huge, unhealthy swallow of her scalding hot coffee, resulting in her windpipe closing and the taste buds on her tongue shrivelling up – perhaps permanently.

"Shit! Tink are you okay?" Tao yelled, darting agilely across the room.

The yummy, dark-haired nymph of Asian descent then began to rub her on the back, directly between her wings. Tink tried her best to speak with the insides of her mouth practically melting and her eyes watering like a waterfall, but inevitably managed to only communicate in duck sounds.

"Did you just quack?" Wendy asked, mirth lighting up her green eyes.

Tink shot her bestie a death glare, along with a middle finger, as she tried to move away from Tao's attentiveness. Tao's personality was as fiery as she was sure his passion was. He was quick-tempered and always the first to step up in a fight. But he was also the first to offer a helping hand and was surprisingly sweet. As evidenced by his continued concern for her self-induced state.

"Here, honey. Have some water," Tao said, taking the glass from Nate, who then also started to gently rub her back.

Wanting nothing more than to rub against their hands like a cat in heat, Tink forced herself to shrug off their attempts to aid her. She gave them a weak smile, offering them a thumbs-up as she sipped on the cool water and sternly ordered her wings to stop their tap dancing. The attempt was futile given she just had two out of three pairs of fantasy-hands touching her, and the iridescent, almost see-through appendages began to beat a frantic rhythm on her back. She saw Nate's eyes focus on them, his irises so dark they were almost black thanks to his Cuban heritage. Tink saw him swallow hard and she wished it was because he found her fluttery wings to be alluring, but alas, she knew that wasn't the case. He was no doubt holding his breath, awaiting whatever powderpuff moment was about to transpire due to her "lack of control".

Although the very blood flowing through her veins was enchanted, her wings were her true source of power, producing pure magic in the form of fairy dust. Despite popular belief, Tink really was very disciplined over her magic. Unfortunately, her wings were the equivalent to a certain male appendage and whenever she was suitably aroused, they took on a mind of their own. It was really fucking embarrassing. Luckily for her, only Wendy and her two human siblings were aware of that little nugget of mortifying information. And Wendy, Jon, and Michael were sworn to secrecy on threat of death. And Tink would do it too – no matter how much she loved them.

Being one of only two females in a motorcycle club full of gorgeous men, Tink had no real vanity in her. She didn't care when the wind made a mess of her hair when she went riding, or that dirt and grease got stuck under her fingernails when she tinkered with her bike's engine. But her wings were a point of pride to her. They were pretty, and she liked that they were pretty. The three sets of shimmery wings, equalling six in total, almost looked like lace and were decidedly delicate-looking, shot through with pastel threads of latticework. They were limbs just like any other and she could control their movements with a thought – most of the time. But she wasn't like some other magical creatures who could shapeshift and hide them. No, her wings were ever-present and Tink had to keep them folded against her back underneath her clothes whenever she was out in public – unless it was Halloween. It was a pain in the butt and often uncomfortable even though they were extremely malleable. Which was why she never bound them when inside the house. Unfortunately, it resulted in many a magical mishap.

Like the one coming up, she thought to herself as Pan moved in her direction. Pan wasn't as tall or as solidly built as some of the other members of their motorcycle club, but that didn't stop him from being a solid presence of authority. Pan radiated strength and stability, as well as lethality and leadership. It was why he was the President of The Lost Boys. The fact that, in an ideal world, he would have been a king had nothing to do with it. His sinewy muscles bunched and flexed as he stalked toward her with feline grace ... and that's when it happened. She hiccoughed and her wings let out a sprinkle of pink and yellow fairy dust, the glittery magic fluttering to the floor. She never really knew what her fairy dust would do each time it was freed. It was magic and magic often had a mind of its own. Tink had no problem using her magic and shaping it to her will with conscious thought. But when it spazzed out like this, the result was anyone's guess. Thankfully, it was usually always harmless – and often fluffy. Some fairy clichés were clichés for a reason.

The room seemed to hold its breath as the coloured magic hit the floor, immediately morphing the beautiful wooden floorboards into thick, lush grass. *That isn't so bad,* Tink thought, right before two white bunnies sprang from the grass ... and immediately proceeded to go at each other like, well, rabbits. Covering her eyes, Tink groaned, wishing the green grass would swallow her up. Unfortunately, the grass simply continued to cushion her feet softly, even as it offered the perfect bed for the fornicating bunnies.

Peeking through her fingers, Tink saw three pairs of masculine eyes looking on in mirth. The shared humour she could handle, but it was the hints of concern and anxiety that had her turning and leaving the room without a word.

CHAPTER TWO

"Fuck!" Pan slammed the deceptively innocuous-looking paper onto the desk. He wanted to set the thing on fire but unfortunately, fire-manipulation wasn't one of his skills. "Fuck you, you perverted piece of shit!" he snarled at the handwriting and the signature of the vampire at the bottom.

The letter was yet another offer to take Tink off his hands while it was still legally permissible. But not only was the offer crude, crass, and never going to happen for moral reasons, Pan also had personal reasons for rejecting each and every single monetary offer, threat, or bribe he received for the lovely fairy. He didn't want Tink taken off his hands, In fact, he wanted Tink *on* his hands. And his body. And his mouth … and his dick. Groaning, he leaned back in his chair, running his hands through his hair. He knew without looking that the burnished brown locks would somehow settle perfectly back into place as if professionally styled. It was the way of his kind. They were simply different variations of physical perfection. It was both a blessing and a curse. A blessing because it made getting laid ridiculously easy – the whole point of being a nymph. And because the human-dominated society they chose to live in was so heavily based on a person's appearance, it meant he and his Lost Boys wanted for nothing when it came to business. It was how his MC owned and operated so many of the businesses in the small-ish town of Neverland. Though Pan liked to think he and his family's work ethic and street smarts also played a big part in their professional success.

The negative part of being the epitome of physical perfection with the charisma to match, was that people only looked on the surface. Nobody took the time to get to know the real you when one look into your crystal blue eyes resulted in their secret fantasies becoming reality. Who cared about Pan's favourite food when he could make you come with one kiss? As much as he had succumbed to his nature's needs over the years, he rarely felt any guilt because those people were just using him in return. It was rather disheartening and lonely and if it weren't for his family of ten, Pan was sure he would be a solitary, depressed, pathetic excuse for a nymph by now. But his family was amazing and each and every one of them saw more than just what was on the surface. They saw the real him and he saw the real them. He was beyond grateful and lucky and that was why he was not willing to allow any member of his family to be bought and sold like cattle. Let alone the extraordinary fairy called Tink.

"What was the offer this time?"

Pan jerked upright, gaze immediately going to the door where his two lieutenants were taking up space. Pan allowed his eyes to roam over the muscled frames of his best friends. Taking in Nate's distinct Hispanic heritage of dark eyes, long, silky black hair and broad build, as well as Tao's slightly smaller, though just as wide frame, his sharply angled cheekbones, and perfectly tousled dark brown hair, he couldn't help but think; *yeah, physical perfection is right.* The two men had been by his side since they were children. Along with Luca, Aron, Lex, and Caden – they had grown up together and were the last of their kind. Male nymphs were a dying breed. They may have been highly sexual beings, but fertile they were not. Their sporadic sub-fertility could have something to do with the fact that in the past, male nymphs never settled with the one female partner for the length of time required to achieve conception. They never settled with any male partner either, for that matter. At least that had been the case until Jon and Caden. Although, he supposed that was also the case for himself, Nate and Tao. They had been lovers for years, but what had been born out of convenience and their natural inclination for pleasure, had slowly morphed into more. Now, the three of them weren't together simply to feed their biological need for sex. They were together because they wanted to be. Because they liked each other. They respected each other.

They loved each other.

Pan shook his head, knowing that his father was likely rolling in his grave over his son's 'weak emotions'. His late father – the long-standing king of the male nymphs – had been deplorably traditional. He hadn't believed in the softer emotions of love or even like. He believed nymphs were entitled to take anything and anyone they wanted. That they were free to use anyone just because they could. Pan had never been of that mindset and thus, a constant disappointment to his father. That's not to say he could go against his nature. Pan couldn't help the sexual energy he oozed as naturally as breathing. Nor could he deny his body's need to engage in sex or feed off desire. But that didn't mean he was a slut. *Okay,* he admitted, silently. *Maybe a little bit of a slut.* But no more than his nature demanded and it certainly didn't mean he was incapable of feeling love and affection. It also didn't mean he was incapable of loyalty or being faithful. His younger years may have been a revolving door of sexual partners and appetites, but that hadn't been the case for some time. In fact, he hadn't physically been with anyone other than Nate and Tao for almost a year. The same went for the two men as well. He knew many wouldn't believe them – including a certain blonde fairy, who seemed to think they ploughed through sexual partners as frequently as blinking. But it was the truth. They had found a way to balance their body's needs with their heart's desires. And that was the sex club.

Pan and his crew owned many businesses in the relatively small town of Neverland. The residents believed they were simply a motorcycle club and had no idea of their magical natures. Because they were well-behaved and not into anything illegal, the police had no issue with them or even the sex club, although, it had created quite the stir when they first opened it. Club Darling was a classy establishment where people from all walks of life and all sexual orientations and cravings could congregate safely and without judgement. It was made up of three levels; The ground floor was the picture of elegance and innocence. It was decorated beautifully in a mimicry of a 1920s style bar, with splashes of plum, black and silver. Its clientele ran more toward the everyday folk who were just wanting to relax after a busy day at work and perhaps find a legitimate date. The ground floor was the 'vanilla floor' as Tink liked to call it. The fact that it was sandwiched between two other levels that allowed patrons to actively engage in sexual acts on the premises, surprisingly was not a turn-off. In fact, it seemed to make the place more popular. Pan thought it was the combination of taboo and class, and also safety. Getting to the first floor above and also the basement level below was not easy and security measures were extreme – though subtle.

The first floor was reserved exclusively for their magical brethren and the humans who were in on their secret. It was a light space, although it had a series of private booths and rooms where patrons could have privacy with their partners or flavour of the night. The sexual energy on the first floor was always high, but it was subtle and controlled. The rules were very strict and nearly always obeyed. Sexual acts were not allowed in the main bar or lounge area. That was restricted to the basement level only.

The basement admitted a combination of human and

supernatural beings, with all magical creatures under a strict gag order; no magic in public and no talking about magic in public. The lower floor looked more like your cliché sex dungeon, with dim lighting, black and mahogany colour palate, and a vast array of sexual accoutrements, including a huge St Andrews Cross on the curtained stage. There were dozens of private and secure rooms catering to a range of fantasies from BDSM to role play. It was an ingenious setup and a profitable one. But the best thing about Club Darling? Pan and his Lost Boys could do something as innocent as walk around inside the club – particularly the lower level – and the sexual energy, desires, and lustful vibes literally seeped into their pores. The rush that came with sex was absent, but it kept them well-fed and healthy. Pan often equated it to vampires who chose not to feed off human blood but animal blood instead. It wasn't as satisfying but it was nourishing enough to survive on.

"Pan? What's the deal?" Tao repeated, frowning and stepping further into the room.

Pan realised his mind had been wandering and he returned his focus to the papers resting on his desk. He felt his blood boil again as he re-read the words from Christoff, the prince of vampires. Instead of repeating them, he growled, "What do you think it is? It's another ridiculous and degrading offer to become Tink's consort. Just another bastard wanting to bind themselves to Tink in order to 'help' ground her magic. Like they're doing her a favour," Pan spat out.

Nate sighed, slipping around Pan's desk and moving behind

him. Nate began digging his thumbs into Pan's tense shoulders, and Pan couldn't prevent a groan from escaping. Nate gave the best massages and always knew the exact places where Pan accumulated his stress. Pan allowed his head to drop forward as Nate worked out the kinks, his eyes catching the movement of Tao, who sat his fine butt on the corner of the office desk.

"You know I don't agree with any of these arseholes any more than you do. And I'm certainly not a fan of the Committee's laws to force Tink into a bond she has no say in. But you know a consort is inevitable, Pan. It's necessary," Nate pointed out, quietly from behind him.

Pan grunted, refusing to answer. Nate was always the voice of reason. He was calm and steady, always a beacon in a storm. That didn't mean Pan had to like what his friend was saying. Tao, the fiery, short-tempered one of their trio clearly felt the same way because he snorted rudely;

"Fuck that, Nate. Tink can do whatever the hell she wants. We've held back all the offers in the past and protect her just fine. Nothing has to change," Tao declared, crossing his arms over his chest.

Nate gave Pan one last pat, leaning down to place an affectionate kiss to the top of his head. "She's becoming more unstable," Nate pointed out quietly, as if he didn't want the universe to hear the words. "You saw her this morning. She was sparkling all over the place. She created bunnies, Pan. Sex-bunnies!"

All three shared a smile over that before sobering once more. Although, he didn't like it, Pan knew Nate was right. A fairy's powers grew with time. As they aged, so did their magic. And magic aged like wine – growing more potent and robust as the years passed. *And delicious,* Pan added. All magic had a certain flavour to it. At least, it did to nymphs and any other magical being that used their senses to survive, whether it be sight, sound, touch, or taste. It was why the vast majority of offers for Tink were from vampires or other species who consumed blood. Tink's blood was literally enchanted with pure magic. They were all more than aware of the high one received simply being in the vicinity of Tink's magic every day. He could only imagine what it would feel like if someone were to actually consume her blood. Which brought him full circle to Christoff.

"Well, it sure as shit isn't going to be the prince of the vampires. If I rescind my roles and rights as her legal guardian, Christoff is willing to compensate me by way of Tink's magical blood."

Tao frowned, "How is that an incentive? We have access to her blood now," he pointed out.

Pan pushed back from the desk, standing up and pacing the length of his office, situated in what should have been the attic of their grand Victorian home. "Oh, the bloodsucker has the brilliant idea of draining Tink at the same time he's having sex with her. The blood would not only be pure fairy magic, but also imbued with sexual energy. A real treat for nymphs like us."

Tao's eyes darkened to almost black as he clenched his hands, forearms and biceps bulging in his anger. Nate's reaction was almost identical and Pan knew they were all on the same wavelength; no-one was getting their hands on Tink unless she wanted them to. Not only was Tink a valued member of their family, but she was also loved. By all of them. At the same time. The others loved her too, but not in the same way Pan, Tao and Nate did. They were inescapably, overwhelmingly in love with her. She was the sole reason they had all stopped seeking sexual gratification from random strangers. Not only did they not want to sleep with anyone else anymore, but they also wanted to prove their worth to her. Too bad the stubborn fairy hadn't noticed. Pan hoped like hell it had nothing to do with him being her legal guardian. It was all on paper and had no impact on their lives whatsoever.

Years ago, Tink had approached Pan with a loophole in the antiquated laws that stated all fairies must be bound to a consort in order to stabilise their magic and ensure the continuation of the fairy species. The kicker was that the Committee would choose the consort – usually one of their own, power-hungry, narcissistic perverts. The fairy would have no say. What's more, once bound, the fairy would become the property of their consort and said consort could do what they chose with her and everything pertaining to her – including her magical blood and wings. Pan had seen many a fairy shared around – bodily and magically. The thought of such a thing happening to their precious Tink made bile rush up his oesophagus. But Tink had figured out a way to retain her freedom – for the most part. Although still powerful, until they reached full maturity, fairies were still considered in need of a guardian. This was usually the role of a parent or relative and didn't have any real-world applications other than on paper. But Tink had broken her bonds with her parents and instead asked Pan to become her legal guardian. That had been fifteen years ago when Tink was a mere sixteen years old. Legally, Tink was Pan's responsibility. Thus, all the offers he received to absolve his guardianship. Unfortunately, fairies reached their maturity at thirty-two. Tink was a mere three months away from that milestone. After that point, his guardianship would mean exactly fuck-all and Tink would be fair game to become the consort of the first and strongest arsehole to mark and bind her. Or even worse – the man who had been accepted as her future consort by her parents when she had been only twelve years old would step up and force the bond. Though no longer under her parent's rule legally, the steps they had taken when she had been a child were still legally binding. Which meant that technically Tink was already betrothed.

"Maybe it's time," Nate suggested.

Pan stopped his pacing and looked at his friend, "Time for what?"

Nate rolled his deep brown eyes, "Don't be dense, Pan. You know exactly what I'm talking about. Time to tell Tink how we feel."

Pan immediately shook his head, "No."

Nate narrowed his eyes, "Coward."

Pan didn't take the bait, largely because it was true. He was terrified they would lose her completely if they confessed their true feelings and what they wanted from her; to be her consorts. Being Tink's friend was both Heaven and Hell, but it was a damn sight better than nothing at all.

Tao blew out a breath, "Pan is right. There's still time. I say we stick to our original plan and wait for Tink to come to us."

Nate looked pained, "What if she never does?"

"Then it sucks to be us," Pan stated. "But it has to be her choice. It has to be because she wants us, not because she feels obligated."

The words were easy to say, but they were becoming harder and harder to obey. Pan just hoped his feisty, winged, sparkly woman eventually woke up one morning and smelled the nymphs.

CHAPTER THREE

Stumbling from Pan's office in a haze of fury, Tink made it just two steps outside the door before turning to kick the baseboard solidly with a booted toe. Hands balling at her sides, she muttered to herself, "That undead freak wants to drain me like I'm some Big Gulp cup and I'm supposed to be okay with it? Not likely!" She kicked the wall a second time, only harder. "*As venerated Prince of the Vampires, this offer should be considered an honour* – huh!" She scoffed loudly, repeating the prettily worded letter to herself even as the words stuck in her throat. "Honour, my arse, and if that blood-binging leech thinks that just because he's a prince, I'll hand myself over like some magical entrée, he's got another thing coming."

Enraged, she lashed out with her boot a third time, only this time a flutter of sparks also rained down from her wings and hands. The ruby-flecked magic sizzling in the air before disappearing like cinders after a fireworks display. "Why, that slimy, pulse-deficient –"

"Tink? Okay, what did the wall do to you this time?" Luca chuckled.

Overflowing with magic now, Tink spun around, her wings accidently spraying Luca with a shower of the sparkly stuff. "Oh no!" As Luca, the youngest of The Lost Boys, coughed and shook shimmering flecks from his hair, she was immediately at his elbow, brushing him down. "Sorry. You surprised me ..." She bit off further excuses, well aware that she'd just given more credence to the idea that she wasn't in total control of her magic. *Damn it.* She *was* in control of course; her flash of magical temper just now wasn't accidental but more of a controlled purge so that she wouldn't be tempted to turn Prince Christoff into stake-bait. She simply hadn't expected company. "I'm really sorry," she repeated again.

"No harm done. Honestly," Luca assured her.

Luca smiled with perfect teeth and those fresh-faced, golden-boy, good looks Tink knew made ladies and men alike swoon. She also knew from Wendy's wine and girl-talk evenings that Luca's innocent eyes weren't as artless as they appeared and she'd heard many colourful descriptions of his more erotic virtues and his penchant for sexual dalliances in very public places. That was a little difficult to imagine just now because her best friend's sometime-lover currently had a number of daisies sprouting wildly from his hair, transforming his usual golden locks into a rainbow of pink, white and yellow.

"Is something wrong? You're looking at me kind of funny."

Luca inspected his rumpled shirt, patting down the last of the sizzling magic.

"Nope, nothing is wrong," Tink blinked twice then purposely dragged her eyes away from the steadily growing blooms, "Everything is great ..." At least she hoped it was; such a miniscule dusting of magic should wear off in minutes, so if she could just keep Luca away from any mirrors for a short while, he could remain blissfully ignorant of the flower garden springing up from his scalp.

"Everything is so great that you're remodelling this floor of the house one kick at a time?" He glanced unconvinced at the flecks of plaster and paint littering the wooden boards under Tink's feet. "Anything I can help with?"

Luca's eyes were so earnest and filled with warmth that Tink could easily understand Wendy's crush on the guy. In all the years she had known him, Luca had been kind and funny and the sort of guy who was always there if anyone needed anything. In fact, if she hadn't been so intrinsically drawn to Pan, Nate and Tao from the very beginning, she probably would have jumped at her friend's idea that they each sample Luca for a delicious evening and then compare notes. But as it stood now, Wendy had completely fallen for Luca – even if the guy was completely clueless about it – and she had her own hands full juggling raunchy daydreams involving Pan and his two lieutenants; sometimes individually but mostly all together, all naked and with their limbs erotically wrapped around one another, and of course, her. She'd actually gone into Pan's office just now hoping to catch a glimpse of the panty-wetting MC president himself, when she'd happened upon the handwritten letter open on his desk. Pan was curiously absent, especially as he had retreated to the office supposedly to work, but the letter drew her inside like a magnet; the spidery scrawl of cardinal-red script beckoning her to read what she knew must be another so-called 'generous offer' to take her off Pan's hands before her next birthday. And she'd been right. The letter was the third of its type this month alone and more proof, not that proof was needed, that unless she could pull a magical time-slowing rabbit from her spectacular arse, her freedom was fast coming to an end. Still, there seemed no point in burying poor Luca beneath her mound of problems, especially when there was nothing he could do to help, so instead she plastered a smile on her face, saying;

"I thought I saw a spider. Big. Nasty. At least eight legs but maybe more." Then, before he could ask further questions, she continued with one of her own, "Have you seen Pan? After dinner he said he had work to do but I can't find him anywhere."

Luca shifted his feet a little uncomfortably then raked uneasy fingers through his blond hair. When his fingers came away yellow with a dusting of what looked suspiciously like pollen, he frowned, "What the –"

"Spring! Don't you just love it," Tink beamed a little too cheerfully. "That dang stuff gets everywhere … now, about Pan?"

Luca regarded their resident fairy with a sceptical look but acknowledged, "Pan left about thirty minutes ago – he said he needed a drink."

Luca's eyes flashed to the papers clearly visible on Pan's desk and Tink knew he had to have heard about the latest bid on her body and her magic. Well, no-one had bothered to inform her. With her jaw now set in a stubborn line, she demanded, "Where did he go for this drink?"

"Club Darling. Tao and Nate went with him." Luca shuffled his feet some more, "Tink, he was going to tell you …"

Colourfully sprouting flowers forgotten, Tink was suddenly more interested in Luca's demeanour and choice of words than his hair. Her wings flitted nervously as she asked, "Did he decide on a consort?"

"What? No!" Clearly taken aback, those words were said in such haste that Luca practically gagged on them. His eyes met hers seriously, "Pan would never trade you away like a camel at a market, no matter what sort of deal he was offered." Luca shook his head, "He left because he was mad and needed to blow off steam, that's all. The latest letter really pissed him off."

"It did?" Tink trusted Pan implicitly but even she knew they were short on time and options. She hadn't really believed that Pan would just offer her up to a consort but her fear of the inevitable future was always there, lurking. Maybe she should be grateful for the offers, she wondered. Any one of them would likely be better than the alternative of her *betrothed*. The filthy beast would no doubt come knocking when the clock struck midnight on her thirty-second birthday. Shaking off a serious case of depression, the idea that the vampire prince's words had made Pan angry enough to leave the house sent a small thrill through Tink's body even as it tugged at her heart. "I think I might go for a ride," she suddenly announced.

Luca smirked. "Uh huh, and will that ride take you past the club by any chance?"

"Maybe," Tink shrugged, returning the droll look. "I'm also pretty sure that Wendy is working the ground floor tonight – want me to pass on a message?"

"Tell her I'll call by at the end of her shift." Luca turned to walk back downstairs then stopped and idly plucked a flower from his hair. "Oh, and why don't you give her this?" he winked.

CHAPTER FOUR

Wearing a form-fitting black leather jacket and matching pants, Tink leaned into the corners of the winding back road. She could have taken a more direct route to Club Darling but she liked the thrill of fast, tight turns and never quite knowing what might come around the next bend. With her visor up, Tink enjoyed the feel of the night air hitting her face as she took a curve so fast and sharp, her knee was almost skimming the ground. Revelling in the way the bike responded to her simplest touch, she straightened up and let her baby really purr. The motorcycle was custom; stylistically similar to a Triumph but structurally sleeker and much more powerful. Engineered and constructed from scratch by Lex, it wasn't just unique. In Tink's mind it was a monochrome masterpiece. With a possible top speed of four-hundred kilometres per hour and six gears, she'd nicknamed the motorcycle *Bullet* – a term of endearment it more than lived up to. Downshifting to take the next bend, Tink appreciated just how snugly Bullet fit her curves and for a short while her worries vanished; she concentrated on the stars studding the sky and the tar beneath her wheels and let all thoughts of being Prince Fang's latest conquest evaporate.

The ride consumed all of her attention until she reached town and peeled off in the direction of the club. Arriving a little after ten at night, Tink knew the parking lot would be taken by their Friday regulars as well as the weekenders who typically passed through Neverland on their way to the mountains, so she chose to park on the street. Swinging her leg over Bullet and removing her helmet, she looked down the line of cars and bikes parked out front and that was when she saw them; three very sexy motorcycles belonging to Pan, Tao and Nate. Each bike was custom like hers, and each oozed powerful masculinity and sex appeal. In fact, the only thing Tink would prefer to riding her bike, was to ride one of those as a passenger. Usually, she liked to be in control, however the idea of being pressed up against one of her three favourite men, relishing the rumbling from the engine and the delicious points of friction where her body would touch theirs, would be more than enough incentive to have her take a backseat for a change.

With heat spreading through her body, Tink sunk teeth into her bottom lip and tried to gather her composure. Meanwhile, beneath her jacket, her folded wings were fluttering against her back as arousal called her magic to life. *Down,* she warned them. The last thing her powers needed right now was more encouragement and unfortunately sexy thoughts about certain nymphs worked her magic into a frenzy. For just an instant she thought that perhaps coming here tonight was a bad idea but then the side door of the club opened and she noticed Nate. Although silhouetted in a dim rectangle of light, she didn't need to look twice to be certain it was him. Nate's glossy shoulder-length hair would have stood out even if the man wasn't six-foot-three and powerfully muscular. A small squeak of pleasure escaped Tink's lips at the sight of him but the sound was mercifully muffled by the music emanating from the bar. After chatting briefly with security, Tink watched as Nate went back inside and she was left standing fever-hot and flustered on the street; her wings beating as though they wanted to fly at the sexy nymph and rip his clothes off. *Okay Tink, you seriously need to pull yourself together.* And just like that her phone buzzed, successfully dragging her back to reality. Pulling it free from her jacket and checking the display she saw Wendy's name pop up. The message read;

'Where are you? Luca called to say you were coming by ...'

There seemed no point in telling her friend she was just outside perving on her housemate, friend and protector like a total creep, so instead of replying, Tink pocketed the phone and walked into the club. Weaving her way between patrons, Tink navigated plush, plum-hued booths and 1920's style servers to reach the shiny black seven metre bar and took a seat. She didn't immediately see Wendy – knowing her friend, she was probably flirting with a customer or on one of the other two levels checking up on things. Wendy was front of house on the ground level and she spent at least five evenings a week ensuring the club lived up to its reputation as an elegant drinking spot and hedonistic hideaway. *And whatever she's doing certainly seems to work,* Tink thought. This floor of the club was a heady mix of art, music, food and drink perfectly suited to winding down on a Friday evening. The bar served timeless classics alongside brightly-coloured drinks containing as much sugar as alcohol, the atmosphere a far cry from the clandestine subterranean floor that served more as a den of debauchery and quenched baser, more erotic appetites.

"There you are!"

Tink turned her back on people-watching to greet her best friend. Wendy rounded the bar wearing a skin-tight red leather mini just long enough to skim her upper thigh and tonight she'd paired this with a black satin shirt, its plunging vee of a neckline providing just a taste of the impressive assets underneath. As always, her friend was sexually striking but also demure enough to keep things professional. Tink imagined that modesty would stay strong for a total of ninety seconds after Luca walked in the door later this evening. "I just arrived – I was actually parking my bike when your text came through."

"I thought you might have chickened out, after all you haven't been here in a while. How does it feel?"

Tink understood precisely what Wendy was referring to and together they'd nicknamed that night the night of the 'the incident'. The incident had been exactly three weeks, two days ago and she still hadn't lived it down. In fact, the boys in the house used it often as an excuse to give her a good ribbing. Still, only Wendy knew the real reason behind her little mishap – everyone else just imagined she was on the fritz. Studying Wendy's amused expression, Tink informed her straight-talking friend honestly, "It feels okay. Of course, it helps that it's just you and me right now – I'm sure I can ease into it."

"You mean you're not going to catch sight of Tao, Nate and Pan making out in a darkened corner and glitter bomb your magic all over the bar again?" Wendy laughed. "That was fun to watch but the drinks on tap ran hot pink for two weeks. Do you have any idea how difficult it is to serve beer the colour of a flamingo? Here," Wendy added a lime wedge garnish to a drink she was preparing then pushed it across the bar, "try this and tell me what you think."

Tink eyed the neon-blue cocktail with some mistrust. The colour was similar to the highlights running through Wendy's fair hair and the smell was fruity. "Why is it fizzing?"

"It's a personal creation. I'm thinking about calling it *Blue Balls* and putting it on the special cocktail menu on Wednesday nights. See if you can pick up the pineapple notes …"

"Maybe later." As tempting as it was to get blitzed with her best friend and forget her problems, what she needed now was something to calm her down – the key to calm was not a tingly cocktail that might lower her inhibitions and stimulate her magic.

"Are you sure?" Wendy asked coyly, "Because I've heard that if you drink enough pineapple right before you sit on a man's face, it makes your –"

"I've heard that too!" Tink held up a hand and dropped her

voice to a hushed whisper, "But can we please not talk about that here?"

Wendy arched a brow prettily, "Well, aren't you a party-pooper tonight. What's stuck in your craw, sweets? Drink your cocktail and tell the friendly bartender all about it."

And so she did; dutifully, and because she suddenly discovered she wanted it, Tink drank her drink and unloaded all of her crap onto her friend like a dump truck. Draining the glass, she set it down on the bar. "Hit me again." Not only could she taste the lingering pineapple, but it had made her lips and tongue feel all tingly. When the stemmed glass remained on the bar, Tink looked up into Wendy's eyes only to find them livid.

"The no-good bloodsucker actually wrote that?!" She scrubbed the bar top furiously. "Well, that explains the guys' moods when they walked in."

"They were in a mood?" Tink hedged, trying not to sound delighted.

"Pan walked right by without speaking to anyone and a head bob from Nate and Tao was all the acknowledgement they could spare. I've seen happier faces on mermaids and we all know how high maintenance they can be. Your trio of hotness went upstairs by the way, although Nate was just down here grabbing a bottle of whisky."

Tink's eyes flitted to the curved mahogany staircase which led up to the second floor. With her contained wings beating excitedly, she mumbled, "I might just check on them. What do you think?"

she asked.

"Don't look to me for more encouragement." Wendy shook her head. "I've been suggesting you jump their combined bones for a year now!" But she did pass Tink another drink. "Don't forget your Balls."

CHAPTER FIVE

Nate wasn't interested in the whisky or making any sort of small talk. He was however very interested in the way Pan was throwing back drinks as though he only had a day left to live. Nate pursed his lips; given the trauma his friend was currently inflicting upon his liver, he thought that might well be true. He, Pan and Tao had been bound in brotherhood for years and they had been friends and then lovers for a good portion of that time. Throughout everything they always had each other's backs, but this time, Nate was worried that Pan shouldered his burden alone. The latest offer for Tink had certainly done a number on his President and although they all shared his fury and his concern about Tink's future, Pan was her guardian. Ultimately the onus was on him to either give her up to her betrothed, accept a new offer, or better yet, find her a way out of this whole crappy deal.

Arms crossed over his chest, Nate sat back in his chair to study his president's face and marvelled at the way it could be set in such grim lines yet still hold all that sex appeal. But if the scowl darkening Pan's handsome features was anything to go by then Tink was safe; his friend and lover might be devastatingly handsome but he could also be dangerous and it would take a braver man than Nate to cross him when he looked that mad.

And there he goes again. As Nate watched, Pan threw back another shot of the fiery liquid, undoubtedly grimacing at their situation rather than the burn. Their archaic laws were bullshit anyway and although Pan, as their leader, acted like a lone wolf from time to time, there was no way Nate was going to let him believe himself alone in this. Hell, there was no way the three of them would ever let another male so much as lay a hand on Tink, let alone claim her. *Claim her!* he snorted loudly, garnering a quizzical look from Tao across the table. Pan meanwhile was too deep in his own thoughts and liquor to notice.

"You're even quieter than usual." Tao caught Nate's eye and his own chocolate irises sparked hot. "What's on your mind?"

"You know what." Nate returned Tao's steady gaze, "Probably the same thing that's had you nursing your drink for the last hour and has Pan gulping his like a fish."

"I heard that," Pan muttered.

"Well, if there ever was a time to give up being a teetotaller, you've got to admit, it's now," Tao acknowledged, stubbornly finishing his drink.

"I think one of us should keep a clear head."

The shorter man shrugged in a gesture that said *suit yourself* and signalled for another bottle for their table. "We could always go find that vampire sonofabitch and rough him up ... better still, we could locate the sender of each letter we've received in the past month and put them in an arena where they fight to the death."

Nate smirked at his lover, "And what does the winner of that bloody tournament get?"

"Roughed up by us. It's a win-win-win situation."

"How exactly is that win-win?"

"Because the three of us get exactly what we want." He pointed a finger around the table, finally landing on his own chest. "Win-win-win."

"Anything else, gentlemen?" A smiling woodland sprite placed a bottle in the centre of their table. "I also put a bottle in your private room, just in case ..."

Nate knew the pixie was angling for an invite but as appealing as her doe eyes and pouty lips were, that just wasn't going to happen. A long time ago, the three of them would have flirted outrageously with the young woman before taking their time to seduce her, but in recent years things had changed. On this floor of the club, patrons – magical and human alike – were encouraged to enjoy a few drinks and company at the bar and lounge but could then adjourn to a private room should they wish to indulge in something more sensual. Of course, when designing the first floor, certain rooms had been allocated for the owners, and Nate, Pan and Tao had shared a room since the doors opened three years ago – the room was exclusively for their use and no-one other than staff had ever been granted access. Nate knew that all The Lost Boys had similar rooms with Jon and Caden's being just next door. He also wondered if it would help Pan's mood for the three of them to go there now and drink in private; he knew it would only take a few drinks alone, coupled with some sensual suggestions and he and Tao could have their president more relaxed than he had been all day.

"Sir?"

Shit. Nymphs were no prudes but Nate was certainly more modest than his lovers and he hurriedly uncrossed his arms to covertly cover his now straining erection. With the situation in hand so to speak, he turned his attention back to the server standing by their table, "Thank you. If we need anything else, we'll let you know." The sprite's disappointment was evident in her suddenly puckered brow and theatrical sulk but Nate didn't care. Forget the whisky, all he wanted a taste of right now was Pan and Tao. In fact, just the idea of the three of them alone in that room was enough to change his priorities from concerned friend to impatient lover and if he could make his friends happier with sex then why shouldn't he? Beneath the table, Nate felt a knee brush against his and he when he met Tao's eyes, he knew he wasn't the only one on board with this plan. In that instant the pheromones at the table spiked in such a way that even Pan looked up, a smile quirking the corners of his mouth for the first time.

"What the hell are we waiting for?" Tao asked.

Nate was first to rise from the table and as such he was also the first to see Tink walk through the door. The sight of her might have flushed colour into his cheeks but it did more than that for his straining cock; the rush of blood practically jerked it in her direction like a compass needle. "Shit," he murmured.

"What's …?" The words died in Pan's throat as he too caught sight of their favourite fairy.

"Tink!"

Always the first to recover in a pinch, Tao called her over. Tink's smile was genuine as she made her way through the crowd, though Nate could see tightness in her shoulders and small lines of strain around her mercury-coloured eyes. He wondered if it was merely due to being inside the club or if it was something more. Tink didn't work at Club Darling even casually like all of them did. On paper, Pan owned the club but it was Wendy, Jon, Caden and Aron who basically ran the place, with Wendy managing the ground floor, Aron running the first floor where they currently were, and Caden and Jon managing the lower level. It may have seemed strange for a couple to run the most notorious part of the club, but it worked for them. Although Tink frequented the ground floor on a regular basis, she rarely ventured to the top floor, and practically never went below. Nate knew it wasn't because she was a prude or judgmental. It simply wasn't her thing and everyone respected that. The same went for Michael, who operated and managed their café – Marooned. As for Lex and Luca, they worked with Tink at Neverland Motorcycles, the MC's shopfront offering custom bikes, accessories and repairs. Their Tink was one hell of a mechanic.

"We were wondering when you'd be back." Tao motioned her over to their table and always a gentleman, pulled out her chair, gesturing for her to sit, "Drink?"

Tink shook her head, "I already have one."

Nate noticed that although welcoming and warm, Tao made sure he didn't touch Tink in any way. In fact, if any of them so much as brushed against her arm right now, they'd probably go off like a rocket. He for one was already primed and ready to go and the possible addition of Tink to the mix was almost more than his body could keep in check; the only thing he'd enjoy more than taking his two lovers into their private room right now would be to have Tink there with them, sandwiched between all that masculine sexual energy. "Ouch!"

"You okay there, bud?"

This sedately murmured query from Pan did nothing to undermine the force with which he delivered another swift kick beneath the table causing Nate to grunt a second time. Apparently, his president was picking up on his overflow of carnal energy, and speared by a pointed look, he knew he needed to tighten up. Thankfully, the conversation had continued to flow around him. Tao had Tink laughing at something he'd said, and Tink … well, she was practically sparkling and not just in a magical kind of way.

Running adoring eyes over her, he took in the way her jacket hugged her chest and how her hair, currently secured in a long tail down her back, shimmered beneath the lights. He also noticed that her wings were discreetly folded away and on that front everything seemed okay; so far, so good. They all understood that Tink's pure magic coursed through her body and wings like a gleaming yet powerful river. Usually that river was successfully contained, however as Tink drew nearer to her thirty-second birthday they'd all noticed some cracks in the dam. A particular sore spot was her magical overflow here at the club a few weeks ago and although he, Pan and Tao were careful not to bring it up, Nate knew the other guys couldn't resist. It was friendly teasing which Tink seemed totally on board with, but for Nate it was also a reminder that their time was running precariously short.

"Tink, sweetheart. We weren't expecting you this evening. What brings you out tonight?" Nate asked, smoothly integrating himself into the conversation.

Tink raised her eyebrows but didn't comment on the use of the endearment. The three of them had begun to give her small signs of affection with casual brushes of their hands, and terms of endearment months ago in the hopes their affections would be reciprocated. So far, they had been shit out of luck. Tink treated them the same way as she did the others in the MC – like brothers. Nate ground his teeth, frustration levels rising. He understood the need to give Tink time and for them to prove themselves worthy of such a precious treasure, but even his famous patience was wearing thin. He wanted the right to touch Tink whenever he wanted. He wanted the privilege of having Tink on his arm when they walked down the street, so the whole world knew she was taken. He knew Pan and Tao felt the same way and it had nothing to do with the power thrumming in her veins. They wanted Tink to be the centre of their universe.

Nate discreetly looked over Tink's shoulders once more, seeing no evidence of her marvellous wings. He was both relieved and disappointed. Her wings, though fragile-looking, were stunning, and he wanted nothing more than to stroke them. He, nor any of them, had ever had the privilege of touching Tink's wings. A fairy's wings were practically sacred and extremely sensitive, and that right was reserved for a consort only. The thought of some nameless, faceless bastard touching the opalescent lace of Tink's wings had Nate's fist clenching and reaching for the one drink he had been nursing all night. Throwing it back in a single gulp, he saw Tao and Pan raise their eyebrows at him in silent inquiry. Yeah, he was being a hypocrite considering their earlier conversation, but he didn't care. Tink was sitting next to him in all her natural beauty and he needed a stiff drink to get through it without tossing her over his shoulder caveman-style.

Tink shrugged, sipping a blue drink Nate had never seen before, "I spent the evening doing some light reading and then needed to get out of the house. Luca said you were here."

Her voice was casual and her body language gave nothing away, and yet, all three of them winced in unison. A pleasant Tink was a dangerous Tink. One look into her grey eyes to see them turning slowly to quicksilver had Pan holding up a hand in supplication; "Tink –"

"So, when precisely were you going to inform me about the

latest bid on my body?"

Tink's follow up question popped out of nowhere; Pan suddenly spat out a swallow of whisky and Nate's eyes shot up. It seemed like no sooner had he thought about the Tink situation than the topic landed in his lap like a grenade. Eyeballing his choking president and Tao, whose eyes seemed to find the table unexpectedly fascinating, he realised he was left to field this one on his own. Tink recognised this also because her next question was directed squarely at him;

"You had to know I'd hear about it," she pointed out quietly. "I think I deserve to know these things."

Nate nodded stupidly not quite knowing what to say. Had they known Tink would find out, and did they think she deserved to know? Of course. But did any of them want to tell her that the Prince of Vampires had plans to violate her body, drain her magic and then probably pass her around like canapes at a party? Fuck no!

"Tink," he began and almost reached out to touch her when Pan abruptly interrupted;

"No-one told you because this whole fucking concept of property and consorts is bullshit." Pan threw back a final shot of whisky and stood up. "You have to be bonded to stabilise your magic? What sort of crap is that? The Committee just throw this Darwinian shit around every few years to gain more power for themselves. Although frankly, the idea that I could get permanently stuck with someone just so the world's fairy numbers didn't dwindle, wouldn't appeal."

It took about ten seconds from when Pan finished speaking for him to realise he'd jammed his foot squarely in his mouth. Nate saw the comprehension pass over his lover's features but he also watched as Tink's face fell.

Pan, head bowed, scrubbed his skull with two hands. "Tink, I'm sorry! I didn't mean that the way it sounded."

Tink remained silent, staring sightlessly into her drink, her jaw clenched tight.

"I hope not, because to Tink I'm sure it sounded like you resent being stuck as her guardian," Nate pointed out, his eyebrows raised high and eyes wide open. His silent look to Pan said clearly; *fix this!*

"You know that's not true." Pan regarded all of them with a heavy expression, "Tink, you know family is everything to me, and that includes you. You're one of the most important people in my whole world. I only meant that the perverts on the Committee don't care about you – they only want to use you in every way possible …" Pan trailed off, likely realising how awful that sounded too. For one who would be King, Pan wasn't all that diplomatic.

Tink shook her head, her low ponytail of straight, very blonde hair brushing against the leather of her jacket. "Geez, Pan. Would you stop before you hurt yourself?"

An amused smile played at her mouth and Nate released the breath he had been holding. There had been no irreversible damage done tonight with Pan's careless words. Or their actions of hiding the letter it seemed, for Tink continued;

"And I know you would have come to me with the letter eventually. Luca already doused that fire for you guys, don't worry." She smiled more easily this time. "I was pissed when I read it, but not at you. Never at you," she promised.

Pan let out a relieved breath, scrubbing a hand over his face, "I'm sorry," he apologised yet again.

Tink titled her head to the side, studying him, "I'll accept your apology for your verbal diarrhea, but that's it. None of you need to be sorry about the continued offers. It's not your fault. I'm the one who should be sorry. I didn't fully consider the consequences of my actions when I asked you to be my legal guardian all those years ago. All I saw was an easy way out from under my family's thumb. I didn't consider what a burden I would be to you, or what danger I would bring to the club." Tink looked down, playing with her straw. "I was selfish."

"Hey, no you weren't. You don't have a selfish bone in your body," Nate promised her, placing a warm hand on her knee.

Pan moved over, sitting on her other side, likewise adding a comforting palm to her thigh. "And you are *not* a burden. You're family. Family is never a burden."

Tao sat down on the small table in front of them, reaching out and covering both Nate and Pan's hands with his own, their shared heat hopefully seeping into Tink. "And we don't mind a little danger, honey. We're a motorcycle club – it's good for our image,"

Tao winked, causing Tink to laugh and sink back into the plush cushions.

"So, you're not giving me to fang-boy, huh?" she asked.

All three of them promptly growled, swearing and cursing, even as they all vehemently said no fucking way in hell. "You know we would never give you up. You're ours," Nate declared, squeezing her knee.

Tink went still, her eyes moving back and forth between the three of them. "Yours, huh?" She licked her lips, leaning forward a little and lowering her voice, "Tell me, exactly in which way I'm yours?"

Nate sucked in a sharp breath, glancing at Pan and Tao. Was it his imagination or was Tink flirting with them? They had waited so long for her to show any signs of interest that Nate found himself struck dumb, unable to form the simplest of words. Fortunately, Tao didn't have the same problem, the bold nymph eyeing her appreciatively before replying on their behalf;

"Any way you want to be."

Tink reclined lazily now, making no move to remove their lingering hands, her eyes peering at each of them, and there was no mistaking the heat in them now. Nate felt his pulse accelerate and his dick harden once more to the point of pain. As if by design, all three of them moved in closer, crowding Tink to the back of the lounge. She spread her legs a little more, making room and Nate damn near swallowed his tongue, "Tink ..." he ground out, his head lowering in order to capture her lips for the very first time.

"I brought you another bottle of whisky. And I thought I would also bring a couple of friends."

The purred words were like a splash of cold water, dousing the small embers of potential Tink had just lit. Nate watched her eyes widen as she took in the woodland sprite waitress and two other scantily clad women who looked to be some kind of fae. Tink stiffened and immediately pushed the three of them out of her personal space. She jumped to her feet, splashing blue drink everywhere, "I'll just be going."

"No! Tink, wait. Please don't go," Nate pleaded, unashamed to beg.

But Tink was already shaking her head and backing away, "No. I'm sorry. I didn't mean to interrupt."

"You're not interrupting –" Pan called out. But it was too late. Tink had already fled in a flash of black leather.

"You're fired!" Tao snarled at the startled sprite.

"What? You can't do that!" The sprite responded, looking on the verge of tears.

"Yes, he can. Pack your shit," Pan backed Tao up. "And you two; leave. Now." Pan demanded of the two hopeful fae.

Nate snatched the bottle of whisky up, drinking straight from the bottle. He prayed they hadn't just lost their one chance of having Tink for their own.

CHAPTER SIX

"Stupid, stupid, stupid!" Tink berated herself as she fled Club Darling. Dashing at her wet eyes, she completely ignored the concerned security guard – as well as her bike – as she practically ran down the dark streets.

What had she been thinking? Flirting the way she had … Tink shook her head, feeling her cheeks heat with mortification. Hadn't Luca told her Pan had gone to the club to blow off steam? What had she expected? They were nymphs! Of course they were planning to have sex with a bunch of fae groupies. She didn't even know why she'd lowered her guard in the first place. Maybe it was hearing Pan's true feelings about the laws surrounding her guardianship and consorts. After the initial misunderstanding, his words had brought a flutter to her stomach and a warmth to her chest, and she'd had the idiotic notion that maybe he liked her. That maybe they *all* liked her.

"Stupid!" She berated herself once more, silently cursing Wendy and her blue fruity concoction. *Yes,* she thought, *it was all*

Wendy's fault! Tink was so absorbed in plotting her friend's demise, she didn't realise just how far she had walked until the resounding silence finally penetrated her ears. Stopping and looking around, she realised she had marched herself right into the industrial estate of Neverland. The poorly-lit area was filled with warehouses, factories, and wrecking yards and was as depressing as it was dangerous. Some of the more sinister magical creatures made their homes amongst the twisted metal and pollution, including the vampires – which was just who she needed to run into that night! Spinning on her booted feet, she began to quickly but quietly make her way back to the busier streets when a series of engine roars met her ears. Tink had a moment of relief, thinking the guys had come after her before she realised the engines sounded completely wrong. Squinting against the bright headlights, she was unable to make out the figures straddling the four bikes as they came to a stop just metres in front of her. But their silhouettes appeared big. Really big.

"Um, mind ditching the lights?" Tink asked, shielding her eyes from their combined brightness. All four headlamps turned off simultaneously, leaving Tink in almost startling darkness. "Oh yeah, that's so much better," she grumbled.

"Well, well, well fellas. Lookie what we found. And on our first night in town too."

The deep voice caused Tink's blood to freeze in her veins. She knew that voice, though she hadn't heard it in well over a decade. Zane, president of rival motorcycle club – or *gang* rather – The

Hooks. He was also the man, and Tink used the term loosely, who her family and the Committee had betrothed her to when she was but twelve years old. Tink shuddered, the sadistic satyr was the whole reason why a then sixteen-year-old Tink had plucked up the courage to approach a band of male nymphs for protection and a new life. Not only did The Lost Boys have a reputation as good men, but nymphs and satyrs were natural born enemies and Tink had counted on Pan taking her in for nothing more than to stick it to his rivals. Of course, that had soon proven not to be the case because everything she had heard about them had been true. The Lost Boys were well respected because they had earned it. They were more than just a motorcycle club; they were a family. And they would do anything to protect their family, including going against the Committee's wishes.

Zane stepped closer, his three goons fanning out around her and effectively boxing her in. Not an appealing man some fifteen years ago, Tink noted that the years had not been kind to Zane. His face was lined and weathered, his long, unkempt beard streaked with grey. He was still large and muscly, but there was also a decided paunch to his stomach. But it was his eyes that had Tink shuddering with revulsion. They were small and beady, dark and cold. They held nothing but the sick desire to inflict pain. Then and only then, would they heat up, Tink knew.

"My lovely consort," Zane grinned. "You're looking well."

"I'm not your consort!" Tink fired back, angrily.

Zane tsked, slowly stalking around her, his vile gaze taking her in, "Not yet. But you will be. You're just a few months shy of magical maturity, my pet. Time to fulfil your obligation."

"Go fuck yourself!" Tink snarled.

Zane and his three delinquents laughed. "I'd rather fuck you."

It had been years since Zane had approached her, though she had never forgotten about him. Nor was she naïve enough to believe he had given up on acquiring her. No, she was worth too much to him. With her blood and magic, Zane was under the misapprehension that the satyrs would be made great once again. It was a moronic notion. The satyrs were on the verge of extinction just like the male nymphs and fairies. A little fairy dust wasn't going to prevent the annihilation of his species. In fact, if Pan and the others got wind of The Hooks being on their turf, their doom would be met sooner rather than later. Pan and his crew had dealt with The Hooks twice in the past. Once when Tink had first joined them and again about ten years ago when they had been stupid enough to enter Neverland. Both times, the four satyrs had fled with their tails firmly between their legs. Literally. The creatures were part man, part horse and had the tails to prove it. Unlike Tink's wings though, they could shift to conceal them. Pan had warned them in no uncertain terms what would happen to them should Zane return for her. But satyrs were all kinds of stupid.

"No witty comeback?" Diesel, Zane's lieutenant taunted.

Tink turned her scathing gaze to the dirty, poorly dressed man, "Diesel. So great to see you again. Tell me, is that really your name? Or were you given it because it's what you like to sniff?"

"Why you –" Diesel lunged for her but Zane stopped him with a beefy arm.

"She's mine. But don't worry, boys, I'll share." Zane winked, causing them all to laugh uproariously.

Tink rolled her eyes. It was people like them that gave motorbike clubs a bad name. "As pleasant as this has been, I'm going to leave now," she said, reaching for her phone to press the emergency alert that would instantaneously give her location to every single one of The Lost Boys. But before she could hit the button, Jagger snatched the phone from her hand. Ryder then gripped her upper arms from behind in a painful hold.

"Uh uh uh," Zane wagged his finger at her. "We don't need you calling your friends and ruining our alone time. After all, it's our bonding night,"

Tink felt all colour leech from her face. "What are you talking about?"

Zane reached out, gripping her chin, tilting her head this way and that. "You know, you really are very beautiful. What an unexpected bonus. And what I mean, dear Tink, is that I've come to claim what is rightfully mine. You think I haven't heard about all the riffraff coming out of the woodwork, trying to poach you for themselves? You really thought I was going to allow that? I don't think so. You're mine, little fairy."

Tink yanked her head free from Zane's punishing hold, "I don't care what the laws say or that I was promised to you. I will never be yours!"

"So feisty," Zane mock-growled at her.

Tink struggled to free her arms to no avail, Ryder was simply too big. She was just about to aim a swift kick to Zane's junk when Jagger thrust his own leg out, colliding painfully with hers and knocking it aside. He laughed, "She really *is* feisty. You're a lucky man, boss."

"When Pan finds out you're in his territory, you're dead. And when he finds out you put your hands on me?" Tink allowed a smile to surface as she pictured the carnage, "You're worse than dead."

Zane huffed, crossing his hairy arms over an even hairier chest. Satyrs were almost *furred* all over. "Huh, you think I'm scared of some nymph?"

Tink narrowed her eyes, trying to buy some time. She knew her bike would have been discovered by now and no doubt Pan would have rounded up The Lost Boys and begun searching for her. "I think you're terrified of him. And if he doesn't scare you, there's always Aron."

Aron was the biggest, meanest looking member in their crew. Six-and-a-half-feet tall, with a shaved head and covered in tattoos, he exuded bad boy. Despite being predictably gorgeous, people still literally crossed the street when they saw him coming – the ignorant fools. Aron was the biggest pussy cat out of all of them – unless you pissed him off or threatened his family. Then Aron went from Bruce Banner to the Hulk, and *smash* was definitely his word of choice. Tink was gratified to see Diesel shifting nervously and he leaned over, whispering something indecipherable in his president's ear.

Zane nodded, a leering grin stretching his mouth wide and making him even more unattractive. "You're right. We're wasting time. I was going to take you with me and claim you in private but something tells me we're running out of time. I'll mark you now and worry about the rest later."

"Like hell you will!" Tink yelled, struggling in earnest now. Once she was marked, that was it. She was considered claimed under the current laws and Pan's guardianship would be null and void. It was ridiculous, but one little bite, causing a permanent scar, would make that person her consort and they'd be able to stabilise her magic – as well as draw upon it themselves. Which was exactly why so many people wanted to be her consort. Her magic, although intrinsically benign, was limitless. And in the wrong hands, disastrous.

The four Hooks laughed at her seemingly shitty attempt at escape. Little did they know, all Tink was doing was wriggling enough to free her wings where they were restricted against her back. They may have been pretty and spider-web thin but they were strong – as was her magic. And despite what the rule book said about a fairy having to be thirty-two before they came into their powers, Tink was more than capable of wielding her magic. And this time, there would be no fornicating bunnies or sprouting daisies. Tink felt Ryder loosen his grip just enough that she was able to make her move. Thrusting her head back, she heard the satisfying crunch of a nose breaking right before she heard a howl of pain and rage. Ryder freed her in favour of falling to his knees and cupping his nose as it bled like a running tap. Zane made a mad grab for her, but it was too late. Tink had her wings free within a second and she quickly leapt into the air. She may not have been able to cover great distances like the dragons, but her wings were more than able to support her own weight for a short time.

But before she was able to fly off, a hard hand gripped her left ankle and tugged hard, bringing her crashing back to the ground. Tink coughed as the breath was knocked from her body, but she still managed to push herself to her feet before Diesel could deliver his open-handed blow. The cowardly turd had been about to hit her when she was down! Disliking him immensely, she used the momentum of her wings to propel herself forward and deliver a forceful throat punch. The arsehole choked and gagged, clutching his neck where Tink hoped he was choking on his Adam's apple.

Harsh fingers yanked at her hair, forcing her head back or else risk a broken neck. "You're going to pay for hurting my boys," Zane snarled, spittle hitting her cheek.

"Oh, I haven't even begun yet, arsehole!" Tink clapped her wings together and fire immediately flared up between them. Zane released her, swearing as he attempted to put out the flames that were now licking their way up the front of his body. He was lucky he was wearing leather, Tink thought, otherwise he would have been crispy by now.

Movement to her right caught her attention and she turned to find Jagger holding a gun. "Really? You bring a gun to a magic fight? Where's your self-respect?" Tink taunted, forcing magic from her wings in a shower of pale blue sparks. She quickly fashioned the electric energy into a sort of rope. Without touching it, she ordered it to do her bidding with her mind and was gratified to see it sizzle and slice its way through the air. A resounding crack sounded in the air when her magical whip snapped across Jagger's face, slicing his cheek open and knocking him unconscious in an instant, his gun falling harmlessly to the ground.

Diesel and Ryder paused where they were, obviously reconsidering charging her. *Maybe they aren't as dumb as they look?* Tink wondered. With nothing but a thought, she fashioned her sizzling rope into two small daggers instead. Pointing them directly at her enemy, she warned; "Don't even fucking twitch, or I'll happily run each of you through. Who the hell do you think you are, huh? You think you can come into our town and attack me?"

"I think I'm your consort and you're mine – bitch!"

The ragged voice came from behind her a mere second before her shoulder felt like it caught on fire. Tink cried out, her concentration broken and her metaphysical weapons dissolving harmlessly into a shower of glitter. Her control was shot to shit and a lightning bolt zoomed from the sky, landing with a deafening boom and throwing everyone off their feet. Her ears ringing and her limbs shaking, Tink blinked blinded eyes to find a huge crack in the ground where her wayward lightning had struck. The four Hooks were either unconscious or dead – Tink hoped the latter – but she wasn't sticking around to find out. Seizing the opportunity, she began to run, her movements jerky, before she was able to command her wings once more. Slowly but surely she felt herself lift higher into the sky as she headed for home. Reaching tentatively for her right shoulder, she felt the bloody wound … and almost fell from the sky when she recognised it for what it was; a mating mark.

Tink had been claimed.

CHAPTER SEVEN

Tink shivered and shook despite the almost scalding heat from the showerheads above her. She had somehow managed to make it home and had promptly stripped herself of her ruined clothing before jumping into her shower. She had all six showerheads turned on and aimed directly at her. From her position on the tiled floor, she had watched as the dirt and grime was washed away, leaving only a persistent pink tinge circling the drain. The wound in her shoulder was not closing up and it throbbed painfully with every beat of her heart. Wrapping her arms around her raised knees, Tink barely stopped herself from screaming. She had been bitten and marked. She had been claimed by *Zane!*

Muffled words caught her attention long enough to stop her mind swirling into madness. She had locked herself into her ensuite bathroom but judging by the pounding on the door, she had little time left to contemplate her newly acquired consort. Sure enough, one voice rose above the others; "Tink! Open this door right fucking now, or I'll knock it down!"

Pan's voice brought tears to her eyes. He would never be hers now. None of them would be. Had she been thinking clearly, she wouldn't have even returned to the great Victorian house nestled happily amongst the trees on their huge acreage of land. She should have just flown off, tried to outrun Zane – who would be coming for what was now officially his. Tink knew he would stop at nothing now and her entire family was in mortal danger. There would be no aid from the magical community because Tink was lawfully bound to Zane and it would be Pan and the others who would be breaking the law if they failed to hand her over. "What am I going to do, what am I going to do?" she repeated as she rocked back and forth.

A sudden crash caused her to flinch and she stared dispassionately through the steam as seven nymphs and three humans tried their damnedest to crowd into her bathroom at the same time. She didn't bother to move, simply watched them as they came to a grinding halt, faces lined with worry. She knew the exact moment Wendy saw the injury on her shoulder because she gasped, her face going sheet-white. Wendy may have been human but she knew exactly what the wound meant.

"Oh, Tink," came her muted words.

Tink could do nothing more than lower her head in shame. Silence reigned supreme for a few blistering seconds, no doubt as everyone took in the grisly visage of a naked fairy with satyr teeth marks in her shoulder. When nobody moved – or even breathed – Tink peeked a look. She inhaled sharply at the look of utter despair on Pan's, Tao's and Nate's faces and she knew she had disappointed them the most. It was in that moment that she felt her heart break.

"Get out," Pan's voice was low, barely above a whisper, but Tink had never heard anything scarier in her life.

Nobody moved for a moment, Caden bravely stepping forward, "Pan –"

"I said get out!" Pan roared.

Everyone jumped and began rushing to the door. Wendy cast one last look over her shoulder before disappearing from view, leaving only Pan, Nate and Tao behind. Clearly, his two lieutenants didn't believe the order had been directed at them, for they made no move to leave. Tink didn't move from where she was curled into her tight ball in the corner of the shower. Belatedly realising this was the first time they had seen her naked, she thought about what a waste it was. They were never going to want to touch her again.

A shadow blocked out the light and Tink squinted to find Nate kneeling in front of her, heedless of the water pelting down on him and saturating his clothes. He didn't say anything as he reached out and gently touched her shoulder. She didn't flinch as he quietly inspected the wound. Too scared to look at any of them and with the silence beginning to fray her nerves, she poked at the sore wound and said; "It won't stop bleeding."

"That's because it wasn't sealed properly," Nate said quietly.

That brought Tink's head up and she looked straight at the

beautiful man in front of her with the soft, dark eyes that she wanted nothing more than to drown in. "What …" she cleared her throat of the hoarseness and tried again. "What does that mean?"

Nate didn't answer her, instead he stood up and turned off the taps. A red fluffy towel came into view and Tink was suddenly airborne as she was wrapped in the soft material and held securely against a solid chest. Even though she had never been there before, she knew it was Tao's by scent alone. He always smelled so damn good. She was carried to her bedroom in silence where she was placed softly on her bed and her shoulder given another thorough inspection, this time by Tao.

"Who was it?"

They were the first words Pan had said since his demand for everyone to leave, and Tink figured the subject matter didn't bode well. Looking over Tao's shoulder and into his blue eyes, she saw rage like never before. But it was the hurt in them that would have had her dropping to her knees had she not already been seated. "Zane," was all she said. It was all she needed to say for them to fully understand what had happened. Despite his desolate eyes and the seething rage contorting Pan's handsome face, his voice was moderately calm as he said;

"A mating mark over the top, one that was sealed properly could perhaps override it."

"Three would be even better," Tao stated, immediately catching on. He looked to Nate for confirmation.

The Cuban nodded. "We can't wait much longer. If we have

any chance of this working then we need to act now."

"Wait ... what? Three what? Three mating marks? Surely you aren't suggesting ..." Tink trailed off because holy fuck, that was exactly what they were suggesting. They wanted to place their own bite over the top of Zane's in the hopes it would supersede his claim?

Tao sat down gently beside her on the bed, careful not to brush her wings or jostle her in any way. "Tink, I know this isn't ideal, but if we mark you – all three of us – there's a chance we could override Zane's bite. For the sake of time, think of it like a dose of anti-venom; an anti-venom chemically alters a toxin and morphs it into something that cannot interact with the body, and that satyr, Zane," he growled, practically spitting the man's name, "is the biggest fucking toxin of them all."

"So, there's a possibility your mating bites could neutralise Zane's, so that I wouldn't have to become his property, that's really what you're suggesting?" Her head was spinning and still wrapped only in a towel, she shivered. It wasn't cold in her room, but she could feel her teeth beginning to chatter as well. *It's shock,* she thought, *I'm going into shock.* But right now she couldn't give into her body's demands and break down. There was too much on the line for her to fall apart and although she was suddenly hopeful that Pan's idea might work, she was more than slightly worried about the consequences. Wrapping her arms around her chest, she rocked a little to take the edge off her anxiety, all the while thinking about how for the longest time she'd wanted nothing more than to be bonded to the three perfect nymphs before her; she'd just never imagined it actually happening and certainly not like this. Hadn't Pan just said at the bar that he'd hate to be bound out of necessity? And having already been his obligation for the past fifteen years, she detested the idea that he'd be compelled to keep her around forever just to save her from Zane's repulsive clutches.

"Tink, it wouldn't just neutralise the mating bite ..."

Nate interrupted her swirling thoughts with his quiet logic and although she perfectly understood what he was telling her, she sat there, letting him explain.

"It would override it," he continued. "We," he gestured around, "the three of us would become your consorts."

"Although that's not guaranteed," Pan interjected quickly. "I can't promise you that this will work but either way we're running out of time to try. That bite *will* seal itself eventually."

They were worried she was running out of time? A small bubble of what had to be nervous laughter rose up and escaped her throat. She'd been slowly running out of time her entire life and now it seemed that time had finally caught up with her.

"Tink?"

There was concern on Pan's face – probably because he thought she was going coo coo for cocoa puffs but his voice held a more urgent query. "What?" she asked sluggishly.

"Yes or no?"

For some reason it took her overtaxed brain a few moments to realise that Pan wasn't asking her if she understood what they were suggesting, he was asking her permission to do it. Hot tears sprang into her eyes and overflowed, running unchecked down her pale cheeks. Pan, Nate and Tao were asking if she was okay with them claiming her; they were giving her back the choice Zane had so callously snatched away. "Yes," she breathed.

What seemed like relief washed over their faces and they wasted no more time on discussion. Kneeling down before her, Pan ever so tenderly shifted the towel so that it revealed her shoulder and the ugly wound she knew looked precisely like a mould of Zane's teeth. He didn't touch it yet but he did lay a gentle hand on her upper arm.

"I need to know if you can sense him?"

At their president's simple question, Tink saw Tao and Nate look away; as though they couldn't bear to see her face when she answered, but Tink understood Pan's reasoning. As a fairy, when she was claimed by a consort, Tink should have been magically tethered to her mate. This invisible leash not only acting as a binding contract but also as a conduit for sensation and emotion. Until now she'd been so panicked that she hadn't considered whether she could 'feel' Zane and the very idea of trying was repulsive. Still, she knew why the question was important and why she had to answer it honestly. If she had a strong tie to Zane already then the likelihood of their plan to save her succeeding, was slim at best. Closing her eyes and steeling herself to what she might discover, Tink searched inside herself for some sense of The Hook's leader, and, just when she was ready to breathe a sigh of relief, she found him. The tether wasn't strong but it existed and through the link she could feel his putrid essence there with her. She gasped, because although he wasn't able to actually touch her, intrinsically they were connected.

"I take it you found him?" Pan's jaw was set in a hard line. "How bad?"

"It's frayed but the link is there." She admitted, trembling in earnest now as though her body could somehow shake Zane loose.

Pan nodded to himself. "Then there really is no more time." He looked to Tink once more and received silent confirmation, then with his hand resting on the back of her head, drew her down to him.

For Tink, the bite was painful and not at all like she had imagined it would be when she had fantasised about this moment so many times over the years. Now the area was raw and tainted and even though Pan was gentle and it was his glorious mouth on her body, she still cried out. Then, in a moment, it was over.

"It's done." He drew back to study her face and in a brittle voice, said, "I'm so sorry, Tink."

"It's okay," she tried to sound positive but her words came out disembodied and frail. Then, because she knew she must, she searched within herself for some lingering connection to Zane. "He's still there," she murmured. Tink witnessed a nod pass between Pan and his lieutenants and Nate moved into range. "Can you still see the original bite?" she asked him.

"Yes." As always, he answered her truthfully. "But not for

long."

Nate was just as careful as Pan when he sunk his teeth into her shoulder, claiming her, but this time she braced herself against the shock of pain, determined not to make a sound.

When he pulled away, Tao, who was still seated on the bed beside her, shared a friendly smile. "My turn. Not how you'd planned to spend your evening, I bet?" Wasting no more time, he covered the remainder of the satyr's bite with his own teeth.

Although the whole ordeal had lasted only a minute or two, when Tao leaned back she swayed and half fell, exhausted into his lap. Without having even the energy to look into their faces, she simply closed her eyes. Still, Tink knew what she had to do before oblivion claimed her. "Zane's gone," she told them after searching within herself one last time for the lecherous satyr. Leaning against Tao's strong chest and with her eyes too heavy to open, she repeated, "He's gone. It worked."

CHAPTER EIGHT

Wrestling with a headache that had nothing to do with the beer in his hand, Zane drank the amber liquid down then scratched his bristled cheek, unsurprised when the tips of his fingers came away soot-black. Even with half his beard singed away, he chuckled darkly, the guttural sound even hoarser due to the heat he'd breathed in during her little fire show and when the bitch's lightning struck. *That fairy-slut sure could pack a punch when she wanted to.* In a corner booth in some no-name dive bar, Zane and his gang were perfectly at home and tonight, thanks to his lucky find, he was in an excellent fucking mood.

Banging on the stained wood table with a meaty fist, he bellowed his order for another round of beers then watched as his lieutenants played a raucous game of pool which involved them smacking the arse of the waitress each time she passed by. Ogling the scantily clad broad, Zane wiped sweaty palms on his pants, wondering if she'd be up for a quick romp in the bathroom before he went and claimed his true prize. Tink might have smaller titties than the bar wench but she was at least two decades younger and she was pure magic. He licked his lips because now her magic as well as her tight titties were all his – he could do with them as he liked, and he had plenty of ideas.

More beers arrived just as Ryder limped around the table to line up his shot and the sight of him made Zane laugh out loud. The fairy had given it to his men pretty good and not only were they beat up but Ryder's nose was flat to his face like the guy'd been hit with a frying pan. Watching him grimace every time he spoke was a fucking delight but he was still looking forward to a time in the near future when they could all exact their own piece of the little fairy – evening the score so to speak.

Zane picked up his pitcher of beer and drank heartily, already imagining all the ways her magic would be useful as well as indulging his fantasies and picturing the first time he would really have at her. Ever generous, he'd pass her around a bit after – everyone could have a taste just so long as no-one touched her wings. Those wings were for him and he'd damn well waited long enough to have them all to himself. It was Tink's greedy parents and his father's position on the Magical Committee, that had secured him Tink when she was but a mere child. The only catch? He'd had to wait until she reached maturity. It had been a risk because her legal guardian could still give her away before then. But all the years of waiting had been worth it. He'd finally sunk his teeth into the delicious fairy.

As her consort, Zane could already sense Tink and he knew

that when he first ran calloused hands over her lace-like wings before he claimed her body, he'd be able to feel that on another level too; her fear, her pain and lastly her acceptance as her body tried to buck him off and failed. She'd know then that she was his. Realising that he could revel in that magical link with his new possession whilst indulging more urgent appetites, Zane was about to call the barmaid over for a tumble when he suddenly noticed that things weren't right; the tether he'd felt since claiming Tink wasn't there. Zane grappled around internally, a metaphysical version of patting his pockets down for lost keys, but the fucking whore was gone. *Gone how?*

"What the hell?!"

There was only one reason he wouldn't be able to sense the fairy and that was if the bond didn't take. Zane snarled, sending a passing patron skittering away; he'd bitten Tink! He'd claimed her but somehow that slippery tramp had gotten away from him again. Zane balled his fists and with one swing of his arm knocked the four beer glasses to the ground. Amid the crash of glass shattering, he yelled at his men, "Fall out, boys! We've got more work to do tonight!"

***

"It worked." Tao repeated Tink's earlier words, his own wonder at their veracity still evident. It wasn't that he didn't believe her; if Tink said Zane was gone then he was, it was just such a miracle that their plan had succeeded that he was still slightly dumbstruck. Added to that was the knowledge that he, Nate and Pan were now her consorts and his joy rivalled his amazement. Tao glanced around at his lovers, not too surprised to see mixed expressions on their faces. After Tink had essentially passed out, they'd left Aron and Lex to guard her door and had moved into Pan's office to talk things through; so far there'd been little talking but a lot of sitting and staring straight ahead. Tao understood that they were all in some degree of shock over everything that had happened but studying them, he couldn't understand why Pan looked so sullen. Whilst Nate was stoic – not an original look for him – Pan's face practically shouted *what-the-fuck-have-we-done* and seeing him that way gave Tao's heart a twist. Sure, the logistics of how it had happened weren't ideal but they'd finally solved Tink's problem; effectively taking her off the market as well as hopefully stabilising her magic. Added to that, Tink was theirs now, something he knew they'd all dreamt about for years; talk about taking down two phoenixes with one stone!

"Why are you smiling like an idiot?" Elbows on knees, Pan looked up from his armchair in the corner.

Tao grinned back at him, "Why aren't you smiling?" Including Nate in his scrutiny, he asked, "Aren't you relieved to finally be Tink's consort? I know I am! Just think, no more pervy letters and offers from guys old enough to be her great-grandfather. She's safe now."

Pan gave a humourless laugh, "Relieved that we just made

Tink our consort because some sick fuck decided to bite her without permission? Relived that we bit her while she was in shock and fear and pain instead of in the throes if passion? No, Tao. I am not relieved!"

Tao sighed, slouching down in his chair. Talk about a mood-killer, his feelings of happiness and joy quickly eroding to worry and regret. "Well, fuck."

Pan snorted, "Eloquent as always, Tao."

Tao clenched his jaw, anger quickly rising to the surface. His hands turned into fists but before he could say or do anything, Nate placed a staying hand on his shoulder.

"Easy guys. You're both right. This should have been a time of celebration. This should have been the best night of our lives. I know it's not how we imagined it, but the most important thing is that Tink is all right. She's ours and she's okay," Nate repeated.

"You're right, Nate. Sorry Tao," Pan said, blue eyes expressing his sincerity more than words ever could.

Tao relaxed, nodding his head and smiling back wordlessly. The two of them often butted heads due to Tao's slippery grasp on his temper and Pan's dominant personality. But Tao loved Pan and respected him as his leader, and they always made up. More often than not, in the most pleasurable of ways. Tao tried very hard to be a gentleman and to not imagine Tink now fully ensconced in that pleasure, as was her rightful place as their consort. It was hard – in more ways than one, he thought as he shifted to ease the ache in his dick. But Pan was right; now wasn't the time. They had a fairy with four bite marks in her shoulder and no doubt, a rival gang about to bust down their doors. Tao could be relieved and happy once they knew Tink was safe.

"Is she safe?"

The voice mirrored his thoughts precisely and was soft and feminine. Considering the MC only had two female members and one of them was currently sleeping off multiple bite wounds, Tao wasn't surprised to see Wendy hovering in the doorway when he turned around. He held out his hands to her and she flew into them, clutching at his shirt and burying her face against his chest. Tao hugged Wendy close, wrapping his arms tightly around her much smaller body. They were all very protective of their two female members, and Wendy, who also had the added vulnerability of being human, was like a sister to all of them. He rubbed her back comfortingly and eyed his president over her shoulder.

Pan sighed, "Well, she's claimed by us, at least. I'm not sure how safe that makes her. But it's a start."

Wendy sniffed and pulled back but remained leaning against Tao. She was quite affectionate, not that any of them minded – nymphs were a rather demonstrative bunch and leaned toward being touchy-feely themselves.

Wendy arched a strawberry-blonde brow, "You think you could say that with a smile? After all, you just got what you've been pining for."

Pan's mouth opened and closed and Tao would have laughed – and applauded considering he had just said the same thing – except he was also in too much shock. *Wendy knew?*

Wendy rolled her expressive green eyes and gave Tao a shove. Crossing her arms over her chest, "Please don't stand there and pretend that you haven't been in love with Tink for years."

Tao watched Wendy tap her foot in irritation, his shocked eyes meeting those of his friends. They had been very careful not to let their true feelings show. Yes, they discussed their feelings with each other and had made their intentions very clear, but they hadn't told anyone else. Not even their other band of nymph brothers.

"Uh ..." was all Tao was capable of articulating.

Wendy snorted, "Gosh, you really are a bunch of men, you know that? You really think it wasn't obvious with the way your lovesick cow eyes follow her every move, Tao? Or Pan, the way you sigh when she talks? And Nate, you literally sniff her hair every time she's near you."

All three of them began arguing their prowess in the art of subtlety, subterfuge and, most importantly, manliness. Because there was no way Tao made "cow eyes" at anyone!

Wendy merely held up a hand for silence, and they all immediately shut their traps. "And what about your sex-drought? You didn't think anyone would notice you've been on the equivalent of a nymph diet for the better part of a year? You three are only having sex with each other because the thought of being intimate with anyone other than the ones you love makes you sick."

Pan finally snapped his mouth shut, "Who else knows?"

"Everyone," Wendy answered, promptly.

"Michael?" Pan asked about the quietest member of their club. "Yes."

"Lex?" Pan then inquired after their redheaded brother who spent the least amount of time at Club Darling.

Wendy continued to stare at Pan as she answered drolly, "Yes. Lex knows. So do Jon, Caden, Aron, and Luca. Everyone knows. As in everyone. Hell, Dean, our postman knows!"

"The postman fucking knows?!" Nate yelled.

Wendy gave a little giggle, nodding her head, "Yep."

"And Tink?" Tao asked, somewhat hopefully. If she knew they loved her then perhaps she hadn't said yes to the bond purely out of necessity. Could it be she maybe felt the same way? But Wendy was shaking her head, looking a little sad.

"She doesn't know. Sometimes we're most blind to the things that are closest to us." Wendy looked each of them in the eye, saying, "Sometimes, we only see what we expect to see. Sometimes ... we're too afraid to look."

Tao frowned, what was she talking about? He was just about to open his mouth to ask when Michael came flying through the door.

"The Hooks just pulled up. And they look pissed."

Tao felt a surge of adrenalin shoot through his body, as well as delight. It looked like another long-held wish of his was about to come true; Zane's head on a platter.

CHAPTER NINE

Tink awoke to a throbbing head and a dull aching sensation in her shoulder. But it wasn't those feelings that had her quickly bolting upright and swinging her legs off the edge of the bed. No, it was the feelings bombarding her from her three consorts. Consorts. Holy Shit! Pan, Nate, and Tao were now her consorts. Reaching up, she brushed her fingers over the large and still-sensitive claiming marks. She didn't need to look at it to know it was a doozy. Four bites within a matter of minutes was sure to leave a whopper of a scar. She hoped only three would be visible to the naked eye.

When three distinct feelings of rage, vengeance and glee, once more bombarded her system, Tink knew that Pan, Nate, and Tao were in the midst of a fight. The sensations of anger and justified retribution emanating from Pan and Nate could mean only one thing; they were fighting Zane. And naturally, Tao was relishing it. Rolling her eyes and cursing, Tink stood up only to realise she was still wrapped in nothing more than a towel.

"Well dammit!"

Given that she was already in her bedroom, plenty of clothing was at hand but she still cursed the damnable few seconds it took for her to get dressed. Zane was here no doubt to take her as he thought was his right and he'd be extra mad if he'd already realised their bond was broken. She wasn't sure that Zane would know she was no longer his yet; after all, their link was tenuous to begin with and the leader of The Hooks wasn't exactly the smartest satyr of the pack. If anything, he possessed just enough brain power to grunt and successfully wipe his own arse at the same time and she suspected the guy had very little grey matter to spare for extraneous reasoning.

With a t-shirt on, Tink struggled into her jeans, hopping and almost toppling sideways as she hurriedly tugged them up her legs. Regardless of if he knew, Zane was still here because of her and she intended to be a part of whatever was currently going down outside. Not that she was worried; The Lost Boys MC had more than enough numbers to take on The Hooks and even without numbers, they were no pushovers. Nymphs might be known lovers but they could fight too and in combat they were fierce. Tink thought that it must have something to do with balance and the yin and yang of the universe; for all their passion and affection, they were equally ruthless in protecting their own.

Even though she was confident that The Hooks were outmatched, Tink still raced out the door of her bedroom and ran barefoot down the stairs, practically running smack-bang into Aron when he stepped into her path.

"Whoa," the gentle giant cautioned. "Easy there, Tink."

Pulling up just millimetres short of his immense chest, Tink puffed, "Aron! The Hooks – they're here." But when her favourite colossus didn't bat an eyelid at that information, she tried again, "We need to get out there." She tried to dash past but Aron simply took a half-step sideways, blocking her exit as effectively as a solid brick wall.

"No."

"No?" Tink's frantic eyes tried to peer past the man's hulking frame to where the front door was wide open but she couldn't see anything. Hauling her attention back to Aron's face, which was a good two feet higher than her own head height, she pleaded; "Please Aron, you have to let me out there. You know The Hooks are here because of me."

"And that's exactly why Pan ordered you to stay inside. Protected."

His voice was so steady and reasonable, just like his dependable nature, that it went against Tink's own nature to argue with him. Then again, there was a time for everything and right now it was time for her to get amongst the action. "Aron, let me go," she ordered sternly.

"No," he repeated, and because he could clearly tell he was frustrating her, offered. "I'm sorry. Sincerely. But those *are* my orders."

Twitching to get to Pan, Nate and Tao, Tink thought briefly

about using her magic or even her wings to dodge Aron's body-barricade but quickly thought better of it; although she sometimes used magic around the house and occasionally – *and accidentally* – sprinkled some of it on her fellow MC members, she would never intentionally hold her powers over them. *Which is just great,* she huffed, *because right now all those fancy principles leave me stranded up shit creek without a paddle!*

At a loss for what to do, Tink reached out across the bond tethering her to her consorts; unlike the fragile link she'd felt with Zane, this union was strong and it took very little effort for her to connect to them. What Tink sensed were churning emotions; a frenzy of tempers and triumphs but also the occasional dull thuds of pain, probably, she realised, because her consorts had started exchanging punches and not just angry words with their rival gang. Of course informing Aron of everything she could sense just now wouldn't make an ounce of difference; obviously he knew The Hooks were here because he'd been told to keep her inside, and he had to also know the encounter could end only one way – with conflict. Given that Aron was not only tremendously loyal, but also had complete confidence in the abilities of his president and lieutenants, the idea of them engaged in a skirmish on the lawn probably wouldn't faze him in the least.

Stuck between a rock and hard place – almost quite literally – Tink decided that it was time to play dirty; not with her magic of course but by resorting to more sophisticated methods.

"Aron," she tipped her chin with as much haughtiness as she

could muster in a pinch, and that wasn't a lot because haughtiness had never been one of her strong suits. "I'm ordering you to move aside."

Aron flexed heavily tattooed biceps as he crossed muscled arms over his chest and shook his head, "I already have my orders, Tink. You know that."

Cocking her head innocently, she prodded, "You have a command from your president and a man who is King of your kind in everything but ceremony, right?"

Aron nodded, seemingly non-plussed. "You see why I can't disobey my orders then … not even for you."

Tink knew that Aron had a soft spot for her. He'd appointed himself to the role of her big brother and over the years had been almost as close a confidant as Wendy, but she also understood that his loyalty to Pan ran oceans deep … and right now, that was exactly what she was counting on. "In traditional nymph culture, isn't it true that women and men are treated equally and that *were* a king to become a consort, his bonded partner would be likewise revered and their orders honoured?"

"Yes. Consorts and their mates are equals in every way, but Tink, I really fail to see how this discussion makes a difference."

Well, duh! Tink mentally smacked her head with her palm, realising that although the entire household knew about the attack on her by The Hooks and the bite mark which marked her as Zane's, Pan, Tao and Nate probably hadn't gotten around to sharing what went down immediately after. Aron wasn't connecting the dots because he didn't know that the three of them had claimed her to eradicate Zane's bite. The man blocking her exit from the house had no clue that he was standing before someone whom in the old ways would be considered his queen. *Well, things are about to get really interesting,* Tink thought.

"Tink, try and be reasonable. Come with me and I'll make you a hot cup of tea," Aron offered her his arm. "I'll even make you peppermint a*nd* I'll put some biscuits on the side."

She stood her ground. "Aron, I am ordering you, as your queen, to move aside." Tink coughed as the words seemed to lodge themselves in her throat but given the furrow deepening between Aron's brows, he'd heard her just fine. *Had she really just called herself a queen out loud? What the hell was she saying? She was a fairy and a damn good mechanic but queen was a stretch. Then again, desperate times ...*

"Tink, what are you –"

Gently tugging the sleeve of her t-shirt down one arm, she showed him her marks. "Tonight I was bitten and claimed by Nate and Tao ... and Pan."

"No shit?" Aron muttered.

"Shit."

Suddenly a wide grin spread over her friend's face, and she didn't know if it was surprise or confusion over his conflicting orders, but Aron stepped fractionally aside. That moment was all Tink needed to sprint for the door and she made it just a few metres outside before hesitating. Until now all she'd thought about was getting to her family but with the force of a WWF smackdown she realised she was also about to come face-to-face with Zane again. Although not a pleasant thought, Tink steeled herself and kept moving. It was close to three in the morning and the acreage around the property was blanketed in full darkness. Trees also surrounded the house, their shadows making the night close to impenetrable. Following her gut as well as her newfound connection, Tink navigated the snaking gravel drive to zero-in on her consorts' position. It took her about forty-five seconds to see motorcycle headlights shining through the trees and just a moment more for the full scene to unfold before her.

Well, she was right about one thing; Pan, Tao, Nate, Luca, Lex and Caden were all engaged fighting The Hooks. That much she'd expected … it was her reaction that really took her by surprise. "Wow," she breathed. In battle, her men weren't just attractive, they were spectacular and Tink felt her nipples and her wings stiffen simultaneously at the sight of them. A light breeze kicked up then, wafting her loose hair over her eyes and obscuring her view. She swatted the pale strands away like cobwebs. *Stop it!* She snapped at the wind, annoyed that it should deprive her of one instant of prime man-candy viewing time. The wind died down instantly and for a few moments Tink stood ogling the perfect masculine specimens in front of her; Pan's strong chest, Tao's muscular denim-clad thighs, Nate's bunching shoulders, and of course, three truly magnificent pairs of arse!

With her wings thrumming an excited rhythm against her back

and pixie dust falling like magical snow, Tink stood awestruck as The Lost Boys fought The Hooks hand-to-hand. As she watched, Nate secured Jagger in a strangling headlock, Tao tripped Diesel and planted a booted foot on his chest, Luca was throwing a series of punches each connecting squarely with Ryder's jaw, and Pan, with a wicked glint in his eyes, was wrestling Zane. The leader of the Nymphs had a bloodied lip, the injury split wide by a vengeful grin but he clearly had the upper hand. *Definite wow!*

Before she exploded into a glitter bomb of magical arousal, Tink decided it was time to make her appearance known … except Zane noticed her first. As he locked eyes with her, raucous laughter erupted from his lungs and contorted his face in a way that was anything but handsome, reminding her of a cackling, gaping wound. Locked in combat with Pan, Tink watched as the leader of the satyrs leaned in and said something by his ear and she watched as Pan's head shot up, catching sight of her. In that moment, Zane seized an opportunity and lifted Pan bodily off the ground before dropping him hard on his backside. Laughing harder now, he towered over Pan whilst making a lewd gesture near his groin.

*Uh oh. Big mistake, s*he winced. *Huge.*

CHAPTER TEN

What the hell was she doing here? Not only was Tink putting herself in danger but just now she was shedding magic like a winter coat! Pan was so shocked to see her that he wasn't fast enough to dodge Zane's meaty hands and ended up flat on his arse in the dirt. With the wind knocked out of him, his ears ringing and the metallic tang of blood in his mouth, Pan cursed loudly. He was actually about to make a run for Tink – his only coherent thought to get her out of there – when Zane made a huge mistake. Locking eyes with Tink, the man made a show of pretending to jerk off and that was when Pan decided he definitely had to kill him. *Kill. Him. Dead.*

Kicking out a foot, he tripped the depraved satyr so that he crash-landed less than a metre to the right. Dazed, it took Zane a second to realise what had happened and by that time Pan was on him. Straddling the larger man, Pan grabbed him by the neck of his shirt and punched him hard with his free hand. He felt the satisfying crunch of bone as Zane's nose squashed against his face and he used that as encouragement to punch him a second time. After pummelling Zane again and again, Pan swore as he was suddenly grabbed from behind and he flailed against his invisible attackers. Realising that pairs of strong arms were dragging him away, he growled at their interference.

"Enough!"

It was Caden's voice by his ear this time and judging by the ring on the second pair of hands, Jon was right beside him. Relaxing somewhat, but only because he would never lash out at one of his brothers, Pan got his feet under him and reluctantly allowed Caden to walk him backwards, away from where Zane's body lay prone but twitching on the forest floor. The man was far from dead but Pan smirked, knowing full well he'd be drinking beer through a straw for at least a month. With help from Luca, Lex, Michael and Aron – who had no doubt followed Tink outside – he noticed that the rest of The Hooks were grouped tightly together, all of them a bloody mess.

"Zane always did have a glass jaw," Caden observed. "But your right hook sure is something."

"I learned from the best." Pan caught Caden's eye over his shoulder.

"Who me?" the older man shook his head. "I'm a lover not a fighter – just ask Jon." He winked conspiratorially at his lover.

"And before Jon, as I recall, you were both." Pan pointed out.

Caden shrugged. "Well, someone had to teach you – it wasn't like you were learning anything in that fortress they called a castle!" He laughed, "I actually thought you might take a swing at me when I dragged you off him. As soon as you saw Tink you attacked Zane like a man possessed – not that any of us could blame you."

Tink! Pan mentally cursed himself with every bad name he could think of. With his head so clouded by revenge, he'd forgotten that Tink was right there, witnessing everything. *And seeing me launch an attack like a wild animal!* If their resident fairy had been unimpressed about taking him as her consort before, he could only imagine her level of regret now. *Stupid. Stupid. Stupid.* Wondering if she'd fled back inside, Pan forced himself to look for her in the dark, but when he laid eyes on her, Tink's expression wasn't one he'd expected to see. *Is that lust?* Although Tink's face certainly held a look he'd never seen before, it definitely wasn't one of shock or disgust. Inspecting her closely, Pan breathed a loud sigh of relief; Tink didn't appear horror-struck or even mildly offended by what she now knew her band of brothers ... *and future lovers?* ... were capable of. If anything, the look was one of awe interspersed with some crazy arousal! And was he nuts or did she just squeeze her legs a little tighter together at the knees? For whatever reason, even from a distance away, his nymph awareness could perceive a heller-strong sex vibe glowing in the aura around their fairy, because apparently his little show of violence had really turned her on!

Storing that interesting titbit away for future reference, Pan gave the okay for Caden to release him, and rolling his shoulders, cast a quick look over their group to make sure everyone was okay. Although a little beat up, they were all standing and even grinning at him like they'd just had the time of their lives.

"Nice job, boss," Lex called out.

Lex actually looked the worst of all of them; an ugly cut beginning just below his elbow and running the length of his forearm, causing his hand to run slick with blood. This was despite the fact that Lex had stayed back as per his orders, allowing Pan and his lieutenants to have first run at The Hooks. He raised a speculative brow at the still grinning nymph.

"It's nothing." Lex replied to his leader's silent query with a shrug and an even cockier smile. "This one," he kicked Jagger's leg out from under him so that the man fell awkwardly onto one knee, "just decided it would be a cool idea to bring a knife to a fistfight."

Pan noticed the shining switchblade feet away on the grass and his knuckles twitched for another round. Lex could easily have been killed and no-one hurt his family and got away with it.

"It's okay … seriously. He didn't even pull it until I was rounding him up." Lex tutted the words like the move was a rookie mistake. "You really should have used this when you had the chance," he told the satyr matter-of-factly.

Giving his friend another once over before being satisfied that Lex was winged but not in mortal danger, Pan wiped his bloodied lip on his arm before eyeballing the sorry bunch before him with a shake of his head, "Not a very sharp play, boys. This is our territory. We've proved that to you before but you gluttons just keep coming back for more punishment." Dropping his voice so that it was low and guttural, he warned them, "Our property, our borders and our fairy." He looked to Tink and received a singular bob of the head. "Told you."

"She was mine. Mine by law!" Zane glared at Pan and the other Lost Boys, "You all know that was my mark on her shoulder – I claimed her first."

"Then perhaps you should have done a better job of it."

Tink spoke for the first time and Pan watched as she strode confidently over to where the bleeding satyr lay, barely supporting his own weight on an elbow.

"Do you often have trouble finishing, Zane?"

"One day you'll learn that I don't!" The Hooks leader snarled and spat at the ground near her feet. "What are you going to do now, little fairy?" he goaded, glaring up at her. "Sprinkle me with your pixie dust?"

Tink cocked her head to one side, considering her options, "You've already seen a demonstration of my power tonight, but I suppose I can cobble together a little something extra."

Now it was Pan's turn to watch awe-struck as, with her wings beating ominously, Tink's shower of magic abruptly stopped, her power instead shooting forth like a burst of sunlight. No bunnies this time, just a rope of what had to be pure, sparkling energy. Tink's magenta lasso sizzled and spat in the crisp night air then lashed out like a snake to where Jagger, Diesel and Ryder were huddled together, effectively enveloping the ragtag group in a ring of flames. The fire seemed to have both a lifeforce and a sense of humour, the blaze circling them in shapes and patterns and alternating between poking out a spitting, fiery tongue to frolicking around as a glowing middle finger. As they were flipped the flaming bird, Zane's lieutenants slumped together onto the grass to avoid the capering heat.

"Now, Zane ..."

As Tink swung her attention back to their leader, Pan noticed a small smile tugging at her mouth but he also saw that her eyes were hard as she addressed the satyr who had claimed her by force.

"I can see you're not in any shape to rise unassisted so please don't get up on my account." She gave him a studious once-over and a look which found him to be entirely lacking. "I merely came out here to give you a warning; if you enter Neverland again, I will cut you. If you ever touch me again, I will cut you. And if you ever, *ever* so much as look sideways at a member of my family again or threaten them in any way, I will cut you so deep you will bleed out where you stand." She knelt beside him and although she hushed her voice to a whisper it still carried amid the night's silence. "My magic will make what Pan just did to you seem like a cake walk – got it?"

She really is amazing. That was Pan's only coherent thought as Tink's dire warning jerked his cock like it was tied to a string. Somehow, in the space of a few hours, she'd not only saved herself from The Hook's attack, but now, when the sensible thing would be to hide away inside, she instead faced down her aggressors, threatening bodily harm if they hurt her family. *We'll never deserve her,* Pan realised, and locking eyes with Nate and Tao he knew they felt it too; each of their faces held equal amounts adoration and infatuation. From across the grass, he wondered if Tink caught an inkling of what was going on inside their combined psyche's because she turned and smiled at them all in turn. And, if he'd thought her power was dazzling then her smile had it beat.

"You'll get what's coming to you, fairy-bitch!"

Pan thought that Zane's breathing sounded more like angry panting now, and he watched as the wheezing satyr tried to rise and failed. Incensed, he slammed a fist onto the ground.

"'You'll pay for this. All of you." Zane hissed.

"What's that, Zane?" By Pan's side, Tao theatrically raised a hand to his ear. "I couldn't understand you through all those broken teeth. Think you can garble that again?"

Pan smirked at his feisty lieutenant but commanded his men, "Let them go." Then, catching Zane's eye, he repeated Tink's warning, "If they know what's good for them, they won't come back. Tink is ours – we claimed her rightfully. There's no mark on her from you." He turned away but not before he saw Tink's magical flames die down just enough that The Hooks could jump over and scrabble to help their leader. He also saw a tiny flame chasing them like a puppy attempting to nip at their heels. "Nice touch," he told Tink, linking arms with her and finally doing what he'd wanted to do all along – lead her back into the safety of the house.

"Thank you." She looked him over, "By the way, you're filthy … I saw the way Zane dropped you on your butt," she teased.

"Just filthy or am I filthy cute? Because *I* saw the way you looked at me when I handed him his arse on a plate," Pan joked wickedly. "And that was all your fault by the way – you distracted me." He raised a brow, another thought suddenly occurring; "How did you get past Aron anyway?"

Tink gave a noncommittal shrug. "I have my ways. Take a shower and we'll talk about it. I think we're going to have a lot to talk about actually."

CHAPTER ELEVEN

Judging by the sunlight streaming in through her bedroom window, it was close to midday when Tink woke up. For a few minutes she still couldn't be bothered to move. Once she was up and moving, she'd be forced to face the day and everyone in the household; most notably the three sexy nymphs who were now her consorts. *Ugh! She had consorts!* Just when she thought things couldn't possibly get any more complicated, lady universe had delivered one hell of a curveball. The upside was that she was officially off the market and there would be no more letters arriving with competing bids like she was some cow to be sold at auction. The downside was that her freedom was officially curtailed by the fact she'd been marked. Not that she thought Pan, Nate or Tao would ever take her liberty away, but traditionally she was now formally theirs … *but doesn't that mean they're also mine?* The stray thought snuck mischievously to mind and Tink had to shake her head vigorously to nudge it loose. That sort of thinking was ridiculous; what had happened last night was simply a union of necessity and she should just be grateful they had offered it without pining for more. *Double ugh!*

Rolling onto her back and away from the sun hitting her between the eyes like a sharpshooter, Tink yawned. Although she'd been asleep-on-her-feet exhausted, those first few hours in bed had been uncomfortable. Every time she'd rolled over or shifted even slightly, her shoulder would ache and wake her, and each time she woke, images and memories of everything that had happened would storm through her mind making it next to impossible to get any real rest. Twisting her neck now to get a better look of her trio of marks, she breathed a loud sigh of relief; at least they were almost healed. As a fairy, Tink didn't possess the power of rejuvenation but a claiming mark wasn't like any other random bite. By claiming her, the mark not only stabilised her magic and intrinsically linked her to her consorts, it also restored the injury in just a few hours. She understood that was why Pan, Nate and Tao had been so quick to act last night; although not fully sealed, Zane's bite would have eventually healed itself, closing over and binding her to him for good.

With a finger, Tink traced three very different sets of bite marks now, none of them resembling the satyr's revolting teeth. Instead, these were marks which during her private fantasy time, before she turned out the lights each night, she'd imagined nipping at her breasts and nibbling their way along her inner thigh. Well, there was fat chance of that now! Not that Tink wasn't serious about bringing her fantasy sex-a-thons to life, but she knew her three crushes had voracious sexual appetites that were part of their biological makeup and that they regularly sought out a new and diverse range of partners ... unfortunately that scenario just didn't work for her. Plus, the idea that some one-time fling might jeopardise the friendship and love between them wasn't something she was willing to risk.

"A penny for your thoughts?"

Startled, Tink shot upright in bed only to see Wendy leaning casually in the doorway.

"I knocked but you were all up in your own head – what's the view like from in there?"

"A little confusing," Tink admitted sourly. "And apparently horny too. Who knew that seeing the men engaged in battle over my honour would be such a turn on?" She smiled and Wendy smiled back.

"Honey, it might be medieval but I've got to tell you it worked for me too. Luca got really lucky last night ... three times."

"Three?" Tink tried to keep the envy out of her voice but knew she failed. "It's really mean to torment me like that," she joked.

"Hey there, sister, you've got three guys all to yourself now. Your own personal harem. Talk about greedy! Have you even done the math on all that orgasm potential? I have and believe me, it's knee wobbling."

"Knee wobbling?" she laughed, imagining that it would probably be next to impossible to stand up after just one round with a nymph, let alone three. Plus, Pan, Tao and Nate weren't just any nymphs – they were extra special and ultra-sexy!

"Down girl. I can see your wings stirring up a cyclone over there." Wendy pushed off from the door and stood by the end of Tink's bed. Reaching out a hand, she dragged her friend to her knees. "Time to get up, sleepyhead," she ordered bossily. "We've got business."

"Business?" Tink asked. "Why? Where?" She knew she sounded a little petulant and whiny but right now she really just wanted to curl into a ball and tug the covers back over her head ... after all, the sun would go away eventually.

"Nuh uh," Wendy cautioned her sternly. "Don't you give me those eyes. We've got business; shoe business. There's a sale downtown and I've been eyeing off a pair of red heels for a month."

"Shopping?"

"And coffee. Coffee first."

Tink wasn't a massive fan of shopping – unless it was for parts for Bullet – but she did indulge in some pretties from time to time. Still, it was the idea of coffee that got her reluctant butt out of bed.

"Atta girl," Wendy grinned. "Let's hit the mall, and over brunch I want you to tell me everything – all the details, leave nothing out."

"What details?" Tink kicked last night's discarded clothes out of the way and rummaged around for clean jeans. "You were at the debrief after Zane and his men rode away – you're all caught up."

"That swine practically crawled away and I'm not even close to being caught up. I wasn't there when Pan, Nate and Tao claimed you and I'm dying to know how that went down." She waggled her eyebrows suggestively.

"Uh, trust me, there was no going down. It was … effective," she decided.

"Effective?" Wendy made a face. "Gross. Tell me there was at least some sexual chemistry in the air?"

Was there? Tink wondered. No one could have called the experience sexy but she supposed there was some little spark inside her each time their teeth laid their mark. Then again, she was half in shock and probably the goosebumps she'd felt were the result of adrenaline leaving her body rather than something more. At any rate, the feelings she had for them weren't going to be enough to change the way the trio felt about her. They might love her but not in the way she yearned for them to and the sooner she admitted that to herself, the better off they'd all be. Dragging her hair back into a ponytail at the nape of her neck, she turned and surprised Wendy with, "Okay, I'm ready to shop. Let's buy those shoes and let's get me a pair while we're out."

"Seriously?" Her friend fist-pumped the air. "Yes! Let's go."

And just like that, Tink found herself being dragged down the stairs.

***

And five long hours later, she staggered, arms full of bags through the front door again. With her feet waving the white flag of surrender and to the faint sound of her credit card company cheering, she barely made it to the couch before collapsing under the weight of her haul. As she glanced despondently down at her array of colourful bags, some small, others larger and over-stuffed with pastel tissue paper, she realised she couldn't remember what was inside half of them. Meanwhile, as she tried to mentally account for her consumer-binge, Wendy was dancing in a circle around the living room, holding her sparkly red shoes high like a prize for all to see.

"Aren't you the prettiest shoes in all the land," she cooed. "We're going to have so much fun together!"

"You do realise that footwear doesn't talk back, right?"

Tao's amused voice carried from the adjoining kitchen and came as such a surprise that Tink felt herself jump. Then, seemingly out of nowhere, there were more of them; Pan, Nate and Luca came through the front door together and Michael entered the living room via the downstairs library. All of a sudden the large space seemed cramped by the smorgasbord of testosterone and Tink found it difficult to breathe. Of course, adding to her breathlessness was the fact that Nate and Pan had obviously come in from the garage and were covered in grease; there were few things more attractive to Tink than grease and muscles and she found herself swallowing hard.

Nate was the first to pull up short when he saw her. "Wait," he held out a cautionary arm to stop his friends progressing any further. "Something's not right."

Tink saw immediate watchfulness enter Pan's eyes and his stance changed from carefree to ready for action. "What?" Her own eyes darted around the room, wondering what the heck Nate was talking about.

He eyed her suspiciously. "Obviously we've walked into another dimension or a body-snatcher has invaded Tink," he informed the other Nymphs calmly. "This one's clearly been to the mall and there is evidence she was shopping."

The collective intake of shocked breaths was amusing but also a little over the top. "Hahaha. Very funny. I'll have you know that Wendy needed shoes and as a woman it was my duty to go with her to buy them. As men, you wouldn't understand."

"She bought shoes but what did you buy?" Tao strolled over, sandwich in hand, to peer inside the largest of her bags. "Oh, I see. You bought everything else."

"Not true," Tink started to fib then gave it up as hopeless. "Okay, okay, I may have seen some earrings I liked … and some new boots." *And the jacket and the gloves and the other earrings that just happened to match the jacket.* "But that's none of your business." Tao merely smirked at her in a way that was so blessedly normal it was hard to believe things had changed last night … and that made her just a little sad. Still, regardless of the banter between the group there was a question which had to be asked;

"Any sign of them?" She was sure the guys would never take The Hooks skipping town for granted and if she knew their methods at all then they'd probably had small patrols scouring the area all day. If The Hooks were still in Neverland, Pan and The Lost Boys would find them, but if Zane and his empty-headed gang had any sense, they'd have left town fast and travelled as far away as possible. Then again, Zane was as thick as he was stubborn and there was a small possibility he'd be dumb enough to regroup and come back for another round.

"We had pairs out this morning searching town – there's no sign of The Hooks anywhere," Nate told her. "Jon and Caden are northside now, checking the warehouse district again but I doubt they'll run into any trouble."

Pan smiled at her reassuringly, "They won't be back. You sent that fire puppy chasing them home, remember?"

Tink summoned a smile of her own but it wasn't easy; apparently the euphoric effects of retail therapy were wearing off. She glanced around the room of expectant faces and lied in a way she hoped was convincing, "Good. I'm glad they're gone and everything can get back to normal." And that was at least half true; she was definitely glad Zane was nowhere to be found, but routine, she realised, wasn't really what she wanted. Still, she was a big girl who had learned a long time ago that she couldn't always have everything she wanted and although a whole lot had just changed for her, it seemed like nothing had changed here at the house. Tink knew she ought to be grateful for the degree of normalcy surrounding her after what had been possibly the most harrowing night of her life, but she couldn't help the rush of disappointment she felt. *What did you expect, Tink?* she asked herself mockingly. *That the next time you saw them, they'd feast on you like a sex-buffet?* In one of her many fantasies, the three of them would beat their bare chests and carry her to bed Tarzan-style, but no-one seemed inclined to do that either. Everything was just ... humdrum, she huffed. Dragging herself to her feet, she announced, "Well, I'd better get these bags upstairs."

Pan nodded. "Remember it's Nate's night to cook. Dinner at seven."

"That's why I'm eating now." Tao saluted his pair of lovers with the last of his sandwich. "The last time you cooked, it was bad, bro." He elbowed Nate playfully in the ribs. "Real bad."

It was bad, Tink recalled. Although how he could stuff up spaghetti and meatballs was anyone's guess. Of course, Pan didn't notice or care because he'd eat anything, but for the rest of them, Nate's night in the kitchen was a struggle to chew, swallow, repeat, and there was a collective averting of eyes around the group as they quickly thought of excuses as to why they'd each be out for the evening – a routine they'd all gone through dozens of times. *Because nothing has changed.*

Scooping up an armful of bags, she nodded. "Great. See you at seven."

CHAPTER TWELVE

Tink sighed, dipping her toe into the pond and turning the water pink. Despite her rather maudlin thoughts, she smiled as the pond began to look like a bowl of sherbet. It had been five days since the attack and her magic came to her now with an ease it never had before. She had always believed she had good control over her magic – and she did. But now she could control it with a mere brush of thought rather than having to concentrate hard to achieve it or expending a huge amount of energy. Her accidental dustings were still just as frequent, unfortunately. But that was hardly her fault; she was now officially bonded to three male nymphs! Tink sighed again, thinking of Pan, Nate and Tao and the water changed from pink to a dark, turbulent blue.

"Now, that's an interesting take on a mood ring."

Nate's voice startled her so badly she would have plunged into the depths of the pretty but icy pond had Pan's dependable hands not been there to catch her. Tink gasped, clinging to his strong arms as he hauled her to his solid chest. She really wanted to snuggle against the broad, warm width, and simply relax for a while. But Pan and the others had already done so much for her, she didn't want to take further advantage, so she patted Pan once on a very fine pectoral muscle before stepping back. Pan frowned but allowed the movement and Tink mustered up a smile for them. "Hey, guys."

Tao raised an eyebrow, "Hey, back."

They continued to stand there in silence. It wasn't necessarily uncomfortable – Tink had never once felt uncomfortable with them in her life – but it wasn't exactly an easy atmosphere either. Tink cleared her throat, "What brings you guys out here?"

The pond was on the eastern side of their property and was sheltered from the view of the house by a thick patch of forest on one side in the shape of a horseshoe, and open to a sprawling field on the other. It was large enough and deep enough for them all to go swimming in the summer, but other than a few visits now and then from the others in the house, Tink was the only one to frequent the peaceful body of water habitually. She loved the irregular shape of the pond, believing it to be in the shape of a heart when she was in one of her more whimsical moods, and she loved the solace the quiet brought to her. It was like her special place and the others very generously allowed her to have it. It was where she fled to when she needed space or needed to think, or even just to read a good book in solitude. If she wasn't at any of their shops or within the house, chances were she was right here. So she wasn't surprised that the boys new exactly where to find her. Although, with the bond in place, they could now pinpoint her location with a mere thought anyway. The water behind her churned a little, the blue water becoming aqua.

Tao looked at the water, "Aqua, huh? I wonder what that colour means."

It meant she was confused. Happy – but still confused. Instead of replying, she simply shrugged and asked again, "What are you doing out here? Did you need me for something?"

"Now, that's a loaded question," Tao muttered, causing Tink to frown in his direction.

Nate gave him a little shove, "What Tao means is that we were looking for you. We could feel you. You're ... sad. Like, all the time." Nate walked over to her and gently held her hands in his, "Talk to us, Tink. You know we can't stand to see you sad, but now that we can feel it too ..."

Tink tugged her hands free, feeling another healthy dose of guilt, "I'm sorry. I –"

"No," Pan snapped. "Don't apologise. And don't feel guilty either. Nate didn't say that to make you feel bad. We just want to help."

Of course they did, Tink thought. *Because that's what friends did.* And therein lie the problem; they were her friends, bound by circumstance and nothing more. "You've done more than enough," she informed them.

Pan shook his head, palm raising to grip her chin and force her eyes to his, "Not nearly enough if you're still feeling sad. Talk to us," he urged.

"I …" Tink took a step back, unable to bear his platonic touch when she knew he would never feel the same way she did. "It's just been kind of a big week, ya know?"

"We know," all three of them answered at the same time.

Tink smiled, they were so in tune. Always had been. All seven of the male nymphs were close, but in different ways. Despite being magical, sexual beings that didn't discriminate, not all of them slept with each other. She knew that Pan, Nate and Tao had only ever been with each other, sharing lovers over their lives, but the relationship with the other four men was purely that of brotherhood. Caden, being the oldest, had placed himself almost in a father figure role and Tink knew that to him the thought of sleeping with any of the nymphs was vulgar – despite their sexual charisma and physical beauty. As for Lex, Luca, and Aron, theirs was an interesting dynamic and Tink wasn't sure where they stood. Though, she suspected it was also intimate in nature.

"Do you regret it?" Tao's question was abrupt.

"Huh? Regret what?" Tink asked, genuinely confused.

Tao shifted on his feet, appearing nervous, "Regret allowing us to claim you."

"No," was Tink's immediate and automatic reply. Although it wasn't how she would have liked things to go, she certainly didn't regret it. Not only had they literally saved her from a fate worse than death, they had fulfilled her biggest wish. Not that they knew that, of course. All three men looked beyond relieved by her quick response and Tink realised she had been a pretty shitty friend to them since taking them as consorts. She had always been able to talk to all of them about anything. Realising she somehow missed them even though they were technically closer now than ever before, she decided to be honest – a little. "I don't regret what you did – what *we* did. I am more thankful than I can put in words. And I don't mean to sound ungrateful, I just …" she trailed off.

"It's not how you pictured your claiming would go," Nate pointed out, quietly.

Tink pursed her lips, nodding her head. Over the course of her life, she had tried very hard not to picture how she would be claimed. Largely because she knew it was inevitable that she would get no say in the matter and she would be irrevocably bound to someone she didn't want – and didn't love. Gaining a consort had always been a negative event in her mind, never a cause for celebration. But though she might be a hard-arse, motorbike-riding mechanic, she was still feminine enough deep down to have allowed a daydream or two to slip through every now and then. And in those dreams, she would picture herself surrounded by joy and laughter and love at the time of her claiming. Her consort – or consorts, rather – would bite her in the throes of passion and bind themselves to her for the rest of their lives not because they wanted to stabilise and have access to her magic, but because they wanted *her*. Because they loved her. Tink shook her head; such dreams were childish. And now? They were irrelevant.

Tao stepped up beside Nate, the three of them making a

formidable wall of masculinity. "Then let us make it up to you," he said.

Tink blinked, shaking her head of the lust fogging her brain. "I'm sorry, what? Make what up to me?"

"Your claiming," Pan replied, softly.

Tink frowned, unsure what they were talking about. There was no going back. For better or for worse, the four of them were bound together for the rest of their lives. "What do you mean? This is kind of a done-deal."

"We know that," Pan promised her before continuing. "What we mean is; let us make love to you."

Tink gurgled, damn near swallowing her tongue. "Make what now?!"

Pan sighed, "The look of horror on your face doesn't really inspire a lot of confidence, sweetheart."

Tink couldn't even close her mouth, let alone speak to reassure him that horror was most definitely *not* what she was feeling.

Nate reached over and gently pushed on her chin, closing her mouth. "Just hear us out, okay?"

Tink nodded, dumbly.

"We're nymphs, Tink. You know desire and sex are a part of our make-up. Sex isn't a taboo act to us or something to be whispered about in the dark. It's just a part of life – a *necessary* part of life," Nate stated, explaining things she already knew.

Oh, now she understood. As her consorts, they were worried

they wouldn't be able to fulfil their nature's need for sex. Being claimed and marked didn't mean you couldn't get it up or sleep with other people. Consorts were free to boink whomever they wanted, though it was considered a betrayal in most traditional claimings. But theirs was anything but traditional and they were no doubt worried they would no longer be able to hold their nightly orgies with random strangers in the private rooms at the sex club. The thought had anger streaking through her body, as well as a healthy dose of pain. She sternly told herself that it wasn't their fault, nor their choice, that they had to feed off desire to survive. But it didn't make it any less painful for her.

Mustering a smile, she said; "Don't worry about it. Nothing has to change, I swear. You know I understand and don't mind your sexy-times with the general populace." She barely got the lie out with a straight face. "This isn't a traditional consort relationship and I won't hold you to those same standards. You're free to sleep with who you choose, whenever you choose," she promised them, even though it hurt her heart to say so.

Pan raised a sardonic brow, "Oh, really? Well, if that's the case then you'll have no problem with us choosing you."

Tao and Nate nodded vigorously and Tink began to feel the first embers of anger "Very funny," she stated, blandly, when it was anything but.

"It's not a joke," Nate assured her.

They certainly did look serious, Tink thought, studying their solemn expressions. And that only served to piss her off even more. They had no idea what their flippant words and casual offer did to her soul. "I don't need or want a pity fuck. Thanks, but no thanks."

Tink went to stalk off, only to brought up short by a very pissed off motorcycle president. "Don't you ever disrespect yourself – or us – like that again. Do you hear me? Do you think so little of us that we would use you like that? We weren't offering a pity fuck, Tink. We want to make love to you. Something nymphs rarely do, I promise you."

Tink felt shame flush her face and she ducked her head, unable to look into Pan's crystalline blue eyes. She *did* know better. But she was just so off balance and their offer had come as a complete shock to her. Good things had been rare occurrences in her life until she had met The Lost Boys, and even then she had known that her time with them was finite. She was going to have to give up her family at some point, whether it was due to a forced bonding or her running away. All her life, she had simply been waiting for the axe to drop, and now that she had some of her dreams coming true, she was still holding her breath and waiting for them to be taken away. Hope was a cruel thing.

Swallowing her pride, she looked up and met each of her consort's gazes, "I'm sorry. So sorry. I didn't mean to insult you. I just want you to understand that I'm okay with who you are. I love who you are – you're my best friends. I would never deny you what you need and I know you need sex. But it's never been with me and it doesn't have to be now. That's all I meant. Honest.

Continue with your normal activities."

Nate's lips twitched but he kept his arms folded sternly over his chest. "And what exactly do you think our normal activities are? Wait, let me guess; sleeping with half the populace of Neverland plus a good portion of the wider world too?"

Tink flicked her eyes between the three prime specimens, remaining silent. Her errant mouth had just gotten her into trouble and she wasn't stirring up more by agreeing with Nate.

Nate snorted, "That's what I thought. Shall we enlighten her, gentlemen?" He asked the others.

Pan rolled his eyes, but at least he was smiling again. Tao's grin was mocking and slightly arrogant, giving him a distinct bad boy vibe that curled her toes.

"You see, dear Tink. The three of us have been in an exclusive relationship for almost twelve months."

Tink frowned, confused. "Exclusive in what way?"

"Exclusive in every way," Pan stated.

Tink was flabbergasted, "You mean you haven't had sex with anyone else? But why? And what about Club Darling? You go there practically every night!"

Tao jammed his hands in his pockets, rocking back on his heels, "We go to the club to feed off the sexual energy there – not to engage in sex. We only do that with each other. As for why, it's because we want to. Because we love each other. Because we are *in love* with each other."

Tink was sure she was doing an excellent impression of a fish out of water, mouth opening and closing, breath expelling in rapid, short pants. They were in love with each other? She knew they were close but she had no idea they were in an actual relationship. She had spent countless nights cursing out the nameless, faceless men and women who she believed had the privilege of touching her men. Yet, for the past year, she had been cursing thin air. She wondered why they hadn't told her and if the others knew, but her more pressing thought was one of guilt. She had just trapped three people in love into a bond with her.

"Before you start with all the guilt again, know that we didn't claim you out of obligation or merely to secure your safety. We love you too, Tink," Nate's voice was earnest.

Tink smiled with warmth, though still a little sadly. She knew he kindly left off the rest of the sentence where he said they loved her but in a different way. Because she knew they loved her like family, like a friend, but it was now more than obvious the love they shared with each other was special. It was a romantic love and something wholly unattainable to her. They were already in love and surely didn't have enough room in their hearts to make space for her – even if they did have the inclination.

"I love you guys too," she told them, leaving off the part where she was madly, disgustingly in love with all three of them and wanted nothing more than to bask in the warmth of their bodies and their hearts for all eternity.

Pan frowned, clearly not happy with her response for some reason, but all he said was, "Okay then. Maybe we should put it this way; we're friends ... right?" He waited for her nod before continuing, "You've been known to have a few 'friends with benefits' relationships in the past ... right?"

Pan appeared to grit his teeth through the last question for some unknown reason to Tink, but she nodded her head. She hadn't been a fan of relationships in the past, knowing what her future held. But she also wasn't a huge fan of one-night stands and casual dalliances were more her style. It had resulted in some short-term hook-ups with guy friends over the years. Most of the time, she had even managed to salvage the friendship on the other side. Though sometimes the guy would become too attached and Tink would have to break all ties. She thought she knew where this conversation was heading now and although a thrilling spark of interest shot through her body, there was no way she would risk their current closeness just so she could see what they were packing between their legs. She opened her mouth to decline their generous offer only to be cut off by Pan.

"Don't say no," Pan quickly said.

"If you don't want to think of it in those terms, think of it the other way," Tao urged. "Did you just hear what Nate said? We love you, Tink."

Nate's dark gaze held hers as he spoke next, "Let us give you the claiming you've dreamed of."

Tink raised her damp eyes and took in the visage before her; Pan, Nate, and Tao stood tall and strong, a solid presence of lust and love and faithfulness all rolled into one unbelievably sexy package. Would it be so wrong to take something for herself for once? To pretend for just one day? Taking a deep breath, Tink finally nodded her head ... and let herself believe, just this once, that they loved her the same way she loved them.

CHAPTER THIRTEEN

She didn't believe them. Pan shared a look with his two lovers and knew they saw it too. All his talk of friends with benefits had been for Tink – so she would feel comfortable sleeping with *them*. Not so she would think that was the context in which they were offering. It seemed to have done the trick because she was currently nodding her head, but it was obvious she had convinced herself that they only saw her as a friend, despite their words of love. *Well, they say actions speak louder than words*, Pan thought, striding to Tink and scooping her up in his arms. Patience at an all-time low from the endless years spent lusting over and loving Tink, he lowered his head, pressing his lips to hers immediately. Pan moaned pathetically, fire coursing through his body and landing directly in his cock. He had been walking around with a semi all week – being able to feel Tink's presence through the bond was a sweet torture. Nate and Tao had been reaping the benefits of all that passion, just as he had theirs. Kissing Tink with everything he had, it took a moment for his lust-fogged mind to recognise the shaking in the body he was wrapped around for what it was; laughter.

Placing Tink on the ground, Pan kept his hands on her waist, pulling back enough to see the mirth in her eyes and as she raised her hand to wipe her lips. Pan winced, they looked very wet. So did her chin. And maybe her cheek. Okay, so perhaps he had been a little over enthusiastic. But he had years of desire sizzling its way through his system, surely she wouldn't begrudge him a little extra saliva?

"Dude, seriously? I kind of thought you'd be an expert at the whole kissing thing," Tink giggled, her silver eyes alight with humour.

Pan grunted, his fingers flexing where they could feel the heat of Tink's skin even through the layers of clothes. Although she was laughing at his expense, she was also relaxed, all hints of previous tension and awkwardness had disappeared. So despite the less than stellar first impression she had of his sexual prowess, he was happy. There was no way any of them would have continued if even a hint of uncertainty had remained. *So, really, I just did everyone a favour*, Pan silently patted himself on the back for a job well done.

"Damn, Pan. You looked like some kind of weird squid. All clingy and sloppy. Step aside, I'll show you how it's done." Tao nudged Pan out of the way, drawing Tink into his embrace.

Pan pouted, crossing his arms over his chest. He would like to see Tao do any better – he cut himself off, because, yes, Tao was doing better. He had wrapped a leather clad arm around Tink's waist, bringing their bodies flush together so not even an inch of air separated them and his other hand gripped Tink gently but firmly by the back of the neck, holding her in place so his mouth could lay pillage to hers. Tink was up on her tippy toes, both hands gripping the collar of Tao's leather jacket, a willing and active participant of the ardent embrace. She wasn't laughing now – and his ego couldn't have cared less. The two of them together was the sexiest fucking thing he had ever seen.

"Sweet mercy," Nate breathed beside him, watching as Tao's hands moved to grip Tink's pert little arse.

Pan gripped his own cock through his jeans, desperately needing relief but happy to prolong the sweet torture of arousal if it meant he got to watch a little longer. He was a tad voyeuristic, a fact that came in handy when you were prone to taking multiple lovers at the same time. And something he was eternally happy for now as Nate stepped up behind Tink and pressed his front to her back. Tink gasped, her body instinctively arching into Nate's huge arousal and Pan had to revise his earlier thought; *now this,* this was the sexiest fucking thing he had ever seen. Tink sandwiched between his two lieutenants.

Pan opened his fly, peeling back the denim just enough to release his hard dick, fisting it almost lazily as he continued to watch. Nate placed a series of kisses over their shared claiming marks and even from a few metres away, Pan saw the way Tink shivered. He knew the still-pink scar would be sensitive and become an erogenous zone now that they were bonded. When Nate reached the underside of Tink's chin, Tao finally released her mouth, allowing Nate to immediately take his place. Tink reached back, gripping Nate's neck blindly and holding him in place. Her other hand still clung to Tao's collar and Pan saw the way his dark eyes fed off the erotic spectacle in front of him. Their eyes met over the short distance, the air practically crackling with sex-fuelled energy. Pan had no doubt that their nymph natures would be well fed that day.

An explosion of colours and a tinkling of chimes, pulled his attention back to Tink, who was looking contrite as her wings beat a frantic rhythm against her back. Pan didn't bother stifling his laugh when he saw Nate's beautiful dark man-bun was now a pastel rainbow.

Pulling on a yellow strand that had escaped its tie, Nate arched a brow at Tink. "I thought your magic was supposed to be stable now."

Tink huffed, crossing her arms over her chest and inadvertently plumping her breasts. Pan eyed the small mounds with the already hard tips, his mouth watering in anticipation of tasting the perfect pebbled peaks. He had always believed Tink had just the right amount of cleavage and was dying to see how her soft flesh fit into his palms. Tink clearing her throat had him refocusing.

"It is stable – and largely was before. I've had good control over my magic for years now."

Pan shared a look of doubt with Nate and Tao but all three were wise enough not to say anything. After all, they were still hoping a foursome was in their near future.

Tink rolled her expressive silver eyes, "You don't believe me."

Tao snaked an arm around her waist, careful to avoid her wings, "Honey, you sparkle on a daily basis. Just yesterday you brought the toaster to life – complete with unicorn horn. You made a toasticorn."

Watching their black, four-slice toaster trotting around their kitchen, its cord swishing madly like a tail, really had been a strange sight. And Pan had seen quite a lot over the years.

"That had nothing to do with my overall magical control. It was my wings," Tink muttered, looking annoyed.

"Your wings?" Nate asked.

Tink looked around, and clearly seeing their confused faces, explained; "My wings sometimes have a mind of their own under certain circumstances. I can't help it. Kind of like you can't always control your man-parts. Sometimes it just stands up and says howdy, right?"

Was she talking about erections? But how would that be the same thing ...?

"Wait a minute ... are you saying you sprinkle fairy dust ... when you're *horny?!*" Nate's voice was shocked.

Tink shifted uncomfortably, shrugging her shoulders and saying nothing.

Nate's eyes widened in incredulity, "But you sprinkle all the time! Like, multiple times a day!"

Tao snorted, "And you call *us* nymphs."

Tink shot them a filthy look, "You literally *are* nymphs! And it's not my fault! All you men prance around the house half naked, looking sexy and smug and exuding sexified pheromones from your pores. What do you expect?"

Pan considered her words and coupled them with her wing-action. He could only come to one conclusion; Tink wanted them. Had wanted them for a long time. His dick – which he belatedly realised was still hanging out of his open fly – jerked. Tink's eyes were drawn to the movement and she licked her lips, her set of upper wings flapping twice. Pan boldly stroked himself, beyond proud and turned on when Tink appeared hypnotised by the sight.

"May I touch them?"

Her eyes flew to his, "I think you already are."

Pan swallowed a smile – Tink's eyes were a little glazed. "Your wings, Tink," he clarified. "May I touch your wings?"

CHAPTER FOURTEEN

"May I touch your wings?"

The words caused Tink to shiver, a shower of gold sparks bursting forth from her back. It was the gruff words as much as the sight before her that caused damp heat to flood between her legs in seconds. Pan certainly wasn't shy about what he wanted – and she couldn't blame him. The man was perfection personified from the top of his light brown, thick luscious hair, right down to his strong manly calves and toes – as well as everything in between. And there was a *lot* of in between, Tink acknowledged, eyeing the huge package on display between Pan's legs.

Her wings vibrated in excitement reminding Tink of Pan's request. Wings were regarded as personal and intimate appendages. They weren't like breasts or testicles or anything where it was considered poor form to walk around with them on display. But they weren't for casual consumption and usually it was only parents and lovers who had the right to handle them. Obviously, family touched them in an affectionate way, whereas between lovers, the sensitive latticework could bring extreme pleasure. Swallowing the drool that had accumulated in her mouth, Tink simply nodded her head. Hell yes, she wanted Pan to touch her wings. She wanted them *all* to touch them, and stroke them, and love them. Kind of how she wanted them to do all those same things to her breasts ... and her thighs ... and everything in between.

Pan didn't even bother tucking his dick away as he strode purposely forward. The nymph king was bold as fuck and Tink couldn't deny how much it turned her on. Raising his hand slowly, Tink held her breath as Pan reached over her back and ran a single finger over her wings for the first time. It was like sticking a wet finger in a power socket, she thought, her entire body erupting with goosebumps. Pan's eyes were locked with hers as his hands began to map every inch of her six separate wings as if memorising their shape and texture. Tink shuddered and moaned her way through the exploration, the sensations a sweet torture.

"You're so beautiful."

Tink's eyes flew open – she hadn't even realised she'd closed them. Pan's words were like a bucket of cold water.

"Tink? Did I do something wrong?" Pan asked, obviously picking up on her change of mood.

"No. You didn't do anything wrong. It's just ..." Tink shifted awkwardly, her gaze meeting Pan's, followed by Nate's and Tao's. "You don't need to say stuff like that. I know you've been with so many women. Gorgeous women. Models even. I'm just me – a too-short mechanic with too-small boobs."

For some reason unfathomable to her, Tink's words caused her three friends to stiffen in anger – she could feel it through their fledgling bond. Their faces turned dark and three unique jaws clenched in annoyance. Although they all clearly had words to say, Pan was the one to speak up, his lieutenants deferring to his lead;

"Firstly, shut up," Pan said flatly, causing Tink to blink in surprise. "Secondly, you're perfect the way you are and there isn't a single thing I'd change about you. Thirdly, what other women? I promise you, I can barely retain basic reasoning when you're in my arms, let alone recall being with anyone else," Pan assured her. He stepped closer, cupping her face between his palms, "You're all I see," he said tenderly.

Pan brought their lips together in a kiss as soft and sweet as the gentle breeze around them. A solid presence at her back informed her Tao had stepped behind her before his lips nibbled a line under her ear on her right, "You're all I feel," he murmured.

Nate crowded her from the left, large, hot hands shaping her waist, soft lips nudging her cheek. "You're all I know," he whispered.

You're all I see ...

You're all I feel ...

You're all I know ...

Tink repeated the words in her head over and over, succumbing into the embrace of her three new consorts. She felt herself melting, the perfectly romantic words causing a different kind of warmth to flood her body and begin to penetrate her closed-off heart.

"Tell us you believe us," Tao urged, his hands rising to shape her breasts.

Tink's heavy head fell back on her shoulders, her eyes meeting Tao's as he peered down at her from behind, "I believe you," she stuttered.

"Thank fuck for that," Tao groaned capturing her lips with his in a deep, messy kiss that had her wanting to rip his clothes off. The feeling must have been mutual because she felt two other pairs of arms fumbling for her shirt and pants.

"Wait, wait, wait," Tink panted, extricating herself from the tangle of six arms. Although she was practically blinded with lust, a series of disappointed groans could be heard. Tink found herself free immediately and quickly heard three different voices asking if she was okay. Prying her eyelids apart, she took in the sight of three, fully aroused male nymphs who had somehow already managed to divest themselves of their shirts and jackets and were nothing but exposed skin from the waist up... and almost orgasmed on the spot.

"Tink? Are you okay? Have you changed your mind?"

Nate sounded like he was chewing glass and that stopping was the last thing he wanted to do. But she knew that he would – they all would – in an instant if that is what she decided. Their consideration and sincerity made her heart go pity-pat at the same time her sex throbbed. Oh no, she had no intention of stopping. But she was feeling an uncharacteristic bout of nerves, and she wanted them gone so she could fully immerse herself into their lovemaking. Taking a deep breath, she admitted, "I'm nervous. You're about to see me naked."

"I sure fucking hope so," Tao muttered, impatience clear in his voice.

The disgruntled look on his handsome face made her smile.

"I thought you said you believed us?" Nate asked, frowning.

Tink held up a hand, "I do. I know you don't say things you don't mean. But this is a big deal. After this, everything changes. You can't un-see me naked," she pointed out.

"Tink, I'm standing here with my dick hanging out. I think our relationship has already entered a new phase," Pan pointed out, clearly unable to understand her female logic. "Plus, we saw you naked five days ago …"

In the shower! How could she have forgotten about that? "That was hardly the same thing!" Tink looked down at Pan's impressive erection, which had been at full mast and proudly waving from his open jeans for ten minutes already and understood that modesty clearly wasn't Pan's thing. But Tink couldn't stop her own apprehension and figured the best way to get it out of the way Rip off the bandaid as it were. "Okay, just close your eyes," she ordered.

"What?" All three men looked incredulous.

Tink rolled her eyes, "If I'm about to get jiggy with my three best friends, I want to do it quickly and I want to do it my way – get it out of the way."

"Get it out of the way?" Nate repeated. "Tink, we're supposed to be seducing you. Giving you the claiming you deserve."

Tink snorted, "Trust me, I'm seduced. Just – do this for me. Please?"

Pan, Nate, and Tao looked at each other with the same expressions of masculine confusion that clearly said they thought she was nuts, but they promptly shut their eyes. Taking a deep breath, Tink reached for the hem of her t-shirt, only to see Pan's eyelids flutter. "Ha! No! Turn around. All of you, turn around. No peeking."

"Tink …" They all moaned.

Tink made a circular motion with her pointer finger, "Turn around while I get undressed or no sexy-times for you."

They quickly spun around, Tao's amused voice reaching her ears easily, "Sweetheart, just so you know. We plan to be all over you – *inside* of you – about ten seconds after you reveal that luscious body of yours. Fair warning for you to savour your bossiness while you can."

Tink felt her breath stutter at the thought of any one of them being *in* her. *Dear gods,* she thought, quickly stripping her outer layer of clothes off. When she got to her plain, serviceable white bra and black knickers, she cringed, making a mental note to amp up her underwear drawer. Hiding the boring garments under the rest of her clothes, she pulled her hair out of its habitual low pony tail and shook the white-blonde strands free. Her hair was long and straight, reaching almost to the curve of her arse. The tiny amount of vanity she had when it came to her looks was reserved for her wings and her hair. And she took pride in the way her hair parted in all the right places, making room for the now-steady wings. Tink threw her shoulders back. It was a simple, adolescent trick to make her boobs look bigger than they were, but it made her feel better. Casting one last look down her bare body, Tink gave an internal shrug, that was as good as it was going to get.

"Okay," she nodded her head, decisively. "You can turn around now."

The men turned as one … and promptly froze. In fact, Tink wasn't even sure they were breathing. Frowning, she looked down at herself once more, wondering if she should have sucked in her tummy. She wasn't really big on exercise and she loved maple syrup and bacon just a little too much. But her magical metabolism seemed to thankfully be enough to keep her naturally in shape. At least, she had always thought so. Maybe she should – "Oompf!"

Tink's breath was knocked from her body, either by the exuberance of Nate's embrace or by his lips stealing it as they closed over the top of her own. His hands wasted no time, mapping her exposed flesh and she gasped into his mouth when he cupped her butt in his hands, bringing her heated core into direct contact with the evidence of his arousal behind his pants. It felt big and now that her nerves had been assuaged she couldn't wait to see and touch every part of him. Pulling back, she smiled into Nate's eyes feeling a little smug from the raw lust on his face.

"I want you so bad," he muttered, breath ragged.

"Yeah, well, you're going to have to share," Pan informed his second in command.

Tink looked around Nate's solid frame to find Tao and Pan completely naked, clearly having made good use of their time and having stripped. Or had they stripped each other? Tink wondered, shuddering at the thought of seeing them together. The only fantasy she's indulged in more over the years than the one where they ravished her from dusk to dawn, was the one where they ravished each other – and she got to watch.

Tao groaned, his cock jerking hard without him even touching it, "What were you just thinking? The spike of lust in the air was incredible."

He licked his lips as if he could literally taste her desire. *And maybe he can,* Tink thought. "I was thinking about you," she revealed. "About all of you … together … naked and together … joined and together … *together* and together." Sure, she was being a little redundant but she wanted to get her point across.

Arrogant, sexy little smirks crossed their faces as Tao and Pan stalked over to her and Nate, the sun caressing their exposed skin and leaving no doubts as to how much they wanted her.

"You like to watch? You naughty little fairy …" Nate's breath tickled her ear as he murmured the words against her skin. Tink swallowed hard and nodded. She heard Nate groan, "Could you be any more perfect for us?"

Tink thought the question was likely rhetorical but that didn't stop Pan from answering. "No, she couldn't." And then, as Tao helped Nate remove the last of his clothing – a sight Tink could stand to see over and over again, Pan dropped to his knees in front of her as if he was going to worship her from the ground up. And in fact, that is exactly what he did.

He started at her feet, before running his slightly calloused hands over her claves and up her inner thighs. Tink trembled when he urged her to widen her stance. She felt very exposed but she was beyond any feelings of reservation now and was fully entrenched in the reality of having Pan between her thighs. When Pan's talented mouth closed over her core, Tink felt her knees buckle, but instead of falling into a graceless heap onto the hard ground, she was wrapped in a strong embrace. Her gasp of pure bliss was swallowed by Tao's mouth closing over hers, even as Nate's hands covered her breasts from behind. It was Nate's forearm holding her up – and holding her immobile. Pan eased a thick digit inside of her at the same time he sucked on her sensitive bud and Tink found herself startlingly close to orgasm.

"Do it," Tao whispered in her ear. "Let us watch that beautiful body come apart."

Tink shook her head, clenching her teeth, not wanting the moment to end. This could be her one and only chance with her three dream lovers and here she was about to come within the first ten minutes. Talk about premature – Tink's inane thoughts broke off with a shout when two other hands joined Pan's where they were dipping and delving and rubbing. Tink arched her back, feeling Nate's teeth glide harmlessly but erotically over her right wing. Ecstasy erupted between her legs, quickly spreading throughout every inch of her body. She cried out, the sound echoing in the clearing around the pond. Tink's keening cry turned hoarse when Tao's teeth sunk into her shoulder, quickly followed by Nate's. She didn't need to look to know they had claimed her directly over their original marks. The two men licked over those very same teeth marks and Tink hummed her pleasure. This time, when her legs refused to hold her up, she was gently lowered – directly onto Pan's waiting lap.

His smile lit up his whole face and Tink didn't need to ask if he had enjoyed himself. It was right there in his sparkling blue eyes. She kissed him, trying to convey how much the moment meant to her without words and figured she did an okay job of it when his hands followed the curve of her butt, over her waist and spine, before gripping her shoulders from the back in an intimate and affectionate gesture. She felt his hand touch the fresh claiming marks and saw his intent in his eyes.

"No," she halted him. "I want you in me when you claim me again."

Pan's eyes flared and she swore his skin glowed prettily as he audibly swallowed, "Are you sure?"

In answer, Tink reached between their bodies, taking his hard flesh between her hands for the first time. Jacking him with a double grip a few times, she was gratified to see the way his head fell back on his shoulders, the cords in his neck prominent as he groaned as if in pain. Dual growls came from her right and Tink damn near swallowed her tongue when she saw Nate and Tao locked in an erotic embrace. Nate was behind the shorter man, one hand tugging forcefully on Tao's nipple has his other hand gripped Tao's gorgeous cock in a firm grip. Tink panted, seeing the two men touching each other in the throes of passion was even better than she could have possibly imagined. Roaming hands captured her attention once more and she saw that Pan appeared just as enthralled by the display as she was, despite the fact he had no doubt seen it – and participated in it – hundreds of times in the past.

She pecked a quick kiss to Pan's lips and smiled as she rose up on her knees where she was straddling the nymph, who was still sitting on his heels on the ground. No doubt the position wasn't the most comfortable for him but Tink knew it would be incredible for her. He would be able to go so deeply this way. Holding his smooth shaft in one hand she sank back onto her knees – and Pan's delicious dick. They both gasped – Tink because the burn and stretch from his entry was an unbelievable erotic blend of pleasure and pain. And Pan because apparently he had gone to Heaven. At least that's what he was muttering over and over.

"Heaven, Heaven, Heaven, I've died and gone to Heaven."

Tink smirked at him, "Not yet you haven't," she promised. Then she started to move. She set a fast pace, her body rising and falling in a furious rhythm as it took Pan in over and over. His body followed her lead and he, oh so generously, allowed her to use him in wicked ways as he sucked up marks on her breasts and gripped her thighs with hard fingers.

Her eyes darted next to them again and immediately met Tao's dark ones. The challenge in them was clear; *use me too, baby*, she swore she heard him say. Her breath was sawing harshly in her throat but she managed to croak; "Suck him."

Tao's mouth quirked and he immediately dropped to his knees, swallowing Nate's thick erection down to the root in one swift move. Nate jerked and swore, his hands lowering to grip Tao's hair as he effectively fucked his lover's face. "Ugh!" Tink knew the sound wasn't actually a word but she had officially run out of those.

"Beautiful, aren't they?" Pan whispered, his breath hot against her sweaty skin.

Tink nodded, wishing she had another set of eyes so she could watch the sexy duo and kiss Pan at the same time. Her hips were losing their rhythm and she could feel herself rushing to peak once again. The feel of Pan's blunt teeth in her shoulder sealed her fate and her body jerked, fingernails digging grooves into Pan's sweaty shoulders as she came in an endless loop. Nate's snarled shout of pleasure captured her attention and both she and Pan turned their heads to watch Nate empty himself down a very willing Tao's throat.

"Sexy bastards," Pan grunted from beneath her, thrusting into her once, twice more before coming with a garbled yell.

Tink felt two new pairs of masculine hands against her back, attempting to soothe and shield. "Tao ..." Tink urged into the ear closest to her mouth, her body awash with pleasure but somehow still needing more. Tao groaned, his hot breaths panting against her back as he rutted seemingly without thought against her body. "Tink, we don't expect you to take all of us tonight. We have time."

But Tink was already shaking her head, "I want you. I want *all* of you. Tonight. I want to feel you for days." And it was true. They had already claimed her once again as consorts, cementing their bond for all eternity she was sure. But she wanted to experience each of them in the most intimate way possible so they would be forever imprinted in her mind and body. Taking her at her word and not bothering to ask if she was sure, Tao proceeded to make love to her with as much abandon as Pan, followed swiftly by Nate. The two other men who weren't sharing her body at the time remained active participants, showering her with kisses and caresses until Tink didn't know whose hands were whose. And she didn't care.

She just wanted them to never let her go.

CHAPTER FIFTEEN

Sitting alone at his desk, Pan felt fear like he had never known before. It flowed like ice through his body, freezing his insides and stealing the breath from his lungs. The piece of paper he held in his hands was not a letter of offer for Tink as he had become accustomed to over the years. No, it was an official letter from the Magical Committee. It seems Zane's final words of *"You'll pay for this"* had nothing to do with another illegal attack and everything to do with the law. Zane had gone to the Committee and informed them of his claim to Tink. He had also told them Pan and his two lieutenants had then stolen Tink from him and forced multiple bites on her in order to override his own first – and lawful – claiming mark. Interfering with a claiming was serious business in the supernatural world and the penalties were high. Public floggings and death being among them. In this instance, if found guilty, Pan, Nate, and Tao would experience both and the remaining Lost Boys would be imprisoned for aiding and abetting the crime.

It had been almost four weeks since The Hooks had launched

their failed attack, and though Pan wasn't stupid enough to think Zane would give up so easily, he wouldn't have dreamt the satyr would go to the Committee. The Hooks were a motorcycle gang, not a motorcycle club like Pan's Lost Boys, and they were into all sorts of illegal things. Zane must have been feeling desperate to resort to seeking out the law – despite the fact that his father was a respected member of the very same establishment. Unfortunately, the sick fuck had more than two legs to stand on. When Tink was a mere twelve years old, her father had sold her magic as rights to the highest bidder – Zane – and informed the Committee. The Committee had then made the future consort-bond official, noting Zane and Tink to be betrothed unless a formal claiming took place before she reached maturity. Which was why they were constantly bombarded with other offers. With Zane's formal allegations, Pan, Nate and Tao would have no choice but to submit themselves for trial. The letter didn't say when or how the allegations would be investigated but Pan knew it was just a matter of time.

How the hell was he going to tell Tink?

It had been two weeks since they had claimed Tink for their own a second time. And in that time, the four of them had settled into a new - and sexy - rhythm. Tink now spent most nights in their bed, educating them all in erotic ways. The three of them were male nymphs and Pan used to be certain there was no sexual position they hadn't tried. Tink was proving him wrong. Once her initial reservations had fled, Tink had proven to be passionate and fun between the sheets. She was a dream come true. The only blip in his otherwise perfect world, was that Tink never slept with them. After they had wrung multiple orgasms from each other, Tink would kindly thank them, kissing them on the cheek in casual affection, and leave to sleep in her own bed. She acted like they were doing her a favour or something. It was frustrating as fuck and Pan knew Tao and Nate were feeling it too.

Outside of the bedroom – or wherever else their desires hit – the four of them spent most of their free time together. They talked and played and Pan believed they had gotten to know Tink on a deeper level. He was sure she was starting to have more than friends with benefits feelings toward them. But every time he saw her eyes soften with the beginnings of love, her jaw would clench and she would turn away, making some joke or other. She was keeping her emotions well in check via the bond they shared, so Pan and Nate and Tao weren't getting any clues or reassurance from that direction either. *If only she bothered to check in with their feelings ...* Pan sighed because she stubbornly wasn't doing that either. None of them had tried to convince Tink they were in love with her again. She clearly wasn't ready to believe them. Pan wondered if she would ever be ready, and if they would even get a chance now after reading that letter.

"Pan? We're just heading out with Lex to go to the shop for a bit. You need us for anything?" Michael spoke from the doorway, gesturing to Lex and Luca.

Pan shook his head, scared to open his mouth in case all his frustrations vomited out like the red, hot lava they felt like inside.

Lex frowned, "What's wrong?"

Everything. "Nothing," he told them, casually opening his desk drawer and putting the letter away. "Can you grab chocolate while you're out? Aron ate the last bag of M&M's and Caden almost went full meltdown."

"I swear that guy PMS's harder than the girls in this place," Luca snickered.

"Harder than you when Jon finished the Christmas cookies and you complained all day because you'd only had one?" Lex ribbed him. "C'mon!"

"Hey! Everyone knows those cinnamon cookies are my favourites."

"Enough," Pan held up a hand, shooing them out the door. Thankfully they went, although Lex shot him another questioning look that told him they knew something was up. It wasn't like Pan to keep secrets from his family but he thought Nate and Tao deserved to know about the letter before it became household news. *And Tink,* he belatedly realised with a groan. How was he going to tell her that the Committee might make her take Zane as a consort after all?

***

"The fuck they will!"

Pan had immediately gone in search of Tao and Nate and right now Nate was wearing a brooding path in the floor with his pacing whilst Tao yelled obscenities.

"The Committee is like a cactus – every member is a prick!"

"Can you at least keep your voice down?" Pan muttered. "I'm as pissed off as you are but right now we need to keep cool heads and figure out what to do next."

"We wait," Nate told them evenly. "All we can do is wait for more information and then follow the Committee's instructions. We have to follow protocol ... at least for now."

"You have got to be kidding me?!" Tao snapped. "You expect us to roll over and let Zane win this? You do know what will happen if the Committee rules in his favour?"

"I know, and we'll deal with that if or when the time comes; Zane will never get his hands on Tink because we won't let that happen but until we hear more, we wait," he repeated reasonably. "There's just no other course of action."

Pan watched as Nate dragged agitated fingers through his long hair. He knew his lover's emotions ran much deeper than they showed and he also knew that Nate was right; until they found out more, they had to sit tight and they had to tell Tink. He said as much out loud.

"Tell me what?"

Tink strode in at that very moment, unceremoniously plonking herself down in a chair. Her face was serious.

"What's going on?" she demanded.

"How did you ...?" Pan began, but then he remembered. "The link." Tink seemed to make use of it when it suited her. Pan tried to be grateful for small mercies but why did she have to listen in and feel the bad stuff and not the good stuff?

"Yep." Tink nodded. "And it seems like it's getting stronger every day. One minute I'm about to take Bullet out on the open road and the next I get this overwhelming feeling that you have something to tell me … so what is it? Judging by your sad puppy-dog eyes, it can't be good."

Rather than explain, Pan simply took out the letter. All three of them watched as Tink read, her expression darkening and her usual metallic-grey irises transforming into a swirling thunderstorm of misery. When she'd finished reading, she put the paper down on the desk and just sat there.

"Tink?" Seeing the effect the letter had on Tink apparently sapped Tao of his anger, leaving only concern. He went down on one knee beside her chair and took her hand. "It will all be okay. No-one will believe Zane anyway – I mean, just look at the guy!"

"Tao's right," Nate agreed, "Zane has been in trouble with the Committee multiple times over the years. I'm sure they won't take this claim of his seriously."

When she continued to just sit there, Pan's worry amped up. "Tink?" he nudged. "Please talk to us." But when she looked up, the expression on her face was harder to bear than her silence.

"What have I done?" she murmured sadly. "I should never have come home that night after Zane's attack. I've ruined everything."

"Honey, you haven't ruined anything!" Pan told her firmly.

"And none of this is your fault."

"It is." Her eyes began to fill but she wiped them hastily before any tears could fall. "I've put you all in danger. I'm so sorry."

Pan scanned the faces in the room and saw that Tink's words had broken them all. Through their bond he could sense her bone-deep distress and her belief that she had done something terrible, but amid her turbulent emotions there was no concern for herself. All she cared about was them. That realisation struck Pan as painfully as a fatal arrow to the heart. *She's going to run*, he thought. Making eye contact with Nate and Tao, he saw the same knowledge in their eyes – because they knew her as well as he did.

Pan forced himself to take measured steps in Tink's direction, carefully sitting down next to her. Gripping her chin lightly between his thumb and forefinger, he forced her face to meet his. "Tink, I'm only going to say this once; Do. Not. Run." Tink's eyes widened but she didn't say anything. That was just as bad as a denial. Silence together with Tink was a scary thing. "I mean it, Tinkerbell," Pan said sternly, using her full name – which their family used only under the threat of death. Tink absolutely hated it. But Pan had to make sure she understood how serious he was. And he was; deadly serious. He, Nate, and Tao had imagined themselves in love with Tink before they claimed her and began making love with her. But it was nothing compared to the depth and intensity of the feelings they shared for her now. Tink was *theirs*. They loved her with every fibre of their being and Pan knew any one of them would fight to the death for her health and happiness. He only prayed it wouldn't come to that.

Tink's eyes had begun to darken with annoyance and anger upon hearing her name, but Pan ignored the very distinct likelihood of imminent maiming in favour of getting his point across. "Tinkerbell," he repeated, "I have absolutely no qualms tying your pretty arse to the bed and locking you in our room. All your meals will be brought to you and all your needs catered to by us."

Tink yanked her hand free, "Excuse me? You're coming awfully close to a swift kick in the balls, Pan," she growled.

Pan merely raised a solo eyebrow, unfazed by her anger. Though he did subtly shift so said balls were not in direct range of Tink's knees or fists. "I don't care. Your safety is my priority and it isn't safe for you out there on your own. I know you think you'd be doing the noble thing, luring The Hooks away from us as well as getting the Magical Committee off our backs, but you would only put us in more danger."

Tink scooted away from Pan's hands and pushed past a still-kneeling Tao, saying, "But they are coming for me. Both Zane and the Committee. How would me leaving cause more trouble than if I stayed?"

"Because we would follow you and fight to the death for you," Nate's words were facts and dropped into the room with the weight of a lead balloon.

Pan could feel Tink's distress through their link and knew

Nate and Tao as her consorts, could feel it too. Pan wanted to go to her but it was more important for her to realise the truth of Nate's words and to believe them. Because if Tink were to run, it would mean The Lost Boys were going to war.

"I'm not worth all this trouble," Tink said miserably, as she wrapped her arms around her waist and gazed out the large picture window.

A growl rumbled in Tao's throat as he stalked across the room, yanking Tink into his arms until her body was pressed tightly against his. "You are worth more than all of us combined. As much as we love everyone in our family and would die for any of them, we would follow you into the pits of hell. If you leave, we would have no choice but to follow you and that would put us in even more danger, do you understand?"

Tink blinked and swallowed audibly, "I understand."

"And do you promise not to run?" Tao pressed.

Tink explored his eyes for a moment, searching for something. Pan had no idea what but she obviously found it because she nodded slowly, "I promise not to run."

Tao narrowed his eyes at her from his superior height, obviously trying to discern the sincerity of her words, "Good. I'm glad you see things our way. I was worried I was going to have to spank you."

Tink snaked her arms around Tao's neck, "And that's supposed to be a punishment? Babe, that's an incentive."

Pan, Nate and Tao groaned in unison as arousal spiked the air.

Tink giggled and the much-needed levity was a welcome relief. But Pan couldn't help wondering how long the reprieve would last. Because if there was one thing he knew with absolute certainty, it was that their fairy was made of stubborn.

CHAPTER SIXTEEN

Just who the hell do they think they are?! Tink fumed as she paced in their huge six-car garage attached to the house. Despite the tingle of interest Pan's authoritative voice and Tao's dominant words wrought to her system, Tink was still pissed. Did they think they could boss her around now just because they had claimed her? Or maybe they thought they had extra rights because she was sharing their bed? *Did* they have extra rights because she was having sex with them? Tink groaned, head falling back on her shoulders as she peered up at the ceiling. She had little knowledge about relationships beyond a few shared nights of pleasure or platonic friendships and found herself well out of her depth when it came to the evolving relationship between herself and her three consorts. They cared about her, she knew that, and she believed they would follow through with every threat they made because they didn't make promises lightly. If they said they would rain down hell to keep her safe, then they would enlist the help of the devil to do it.

Tink felt her anger dissipate just that easily. Yes, the feminist in her balked at the men-folk ordering her around, but how could she stay mad at people who cared about her so deeply? It was wonderful, Tink thought, sighing as her shoulders drooped. *It was a gift*, she acknowledged, blinking back tears. And yet, it still wasn't enough and that left Tink feeling beyond selfish and ungrateful. She had three amazing men who were literally willing to go to war for her and yet she yearned for more. She didn't want their sword arms; she wanted their hearts. *Maybe sleeping with them was a bad idea*, Tink thought. She knew physical closeness bred emotional intimacy and she had already been head over heels for them in the first place. Now, three weeks of supreme orgasms, lingering embraces, and shared laughter later and she was in well out of her depth. In fact, as she picked at some stubborn grease under her fingernails, she idly wondered if she would even be able to survive without them in her life anymore.

Shaking off the morose, pathetic thoughts, Tink assured herself she could. Perhaps she would never *thrive* without the three beautiful, male nymphs by her side, but she would survive. Her heart would continue to beat and air would keep filling her lungs. *Because that's how the autonomous nervous system functions. Not because you would want to,* Tink's inner voice pointed out.

"Oh, shut up, you pansy," Tink muttered.

"Who's the pansy?"

Aron's deep, base voice echoed through the garage, and Tink couldn't hold back the smile that lit her face as the gentle giant walked across the large space toward her. Nothing had changed between them since Tink's revelations about Pan, Nate and Tao becoming her consorts and the fact that he ruffled her hair playfully now was a testament to that. In fact, none of the other Lost Boys treated her any differently than they had before and that was a blessing in itself.

"You were talking to yourself again, weren't you?" Aron chuckled. "Classic Tink."

"I was just venting." She spun around and chose a torque wrench from the impressive rack of tools at her back, deciding that if she was here, she might as well work on a bike. The methodical nature of mechanical tasks always calmed her and sometimes she would just kneel here for hours, taking motorcycles apart, polishing and greasing their parts and putting them back together again. They were just like three-dimensional jigsaws, she thought. Big, beautiful, dependable metal jigsaws and for some reason they took her to her happy place. Plonking her butt unceremoniously on the cement floor, she began tinkering with the bike nearest to her; it happened to be Luca's, but in her mind, a bike was a bike and was fair game.

"What's got you so worked up, cupcake? And while you're down there, check fourth gear; Luca mentioned it wasn't transitioning smoothly."

"Can do." Tink straddled the bike herself and tapped up through the gears to get a feel for what was going on, then she dropped back to the ground and got busy. Meanwhile, Aron stood over her shoulder watching her work and using her silence to get her to talk to him. It was his most effective technique; drag a silence out until someone broke it, and she did. Without looking up, she informed him bleakly, "I've gotten you all into trouble. Zane has formally complained to the Magical Committee and now they're investigating the legitimacy of his marking me. If they find out that Pan, Nate and Tao claimed me after Zane – that their bites overrode his – the three of them could end up ..." She couldn't even finish the sentence. The knowledge of what could happen to them and to the other Lost Boys was just too much for her to think about. "It's bad," she finished, defeated.

Aron frowned. "Tink, I don't know what you're talking about but you're rambling. Were you in here this morning when Lex was spray painting the decals on the *Spyder?* Because if that's the case you should probably wear a mask."

Aron's frown was so genuinely confused that Tink had to second guess what was going on between them. "You do realise how much trouble they're in?" she said. "And this could affect all of you." Tink stood and pointed idly to the clutch cables, "It just needs some lubricant. That's why it's sticking."

Aron nodded. "Luca will be happy to hear that. I know he meant to look at it tonight."

"Well, now he won't have to," Tink murmured. Then, because it bothered her that Aron was taking her news so calmly, she demanded, "Why doesn't any of this faze you? You didn't even look surprised when I told you about the letter and you certainly don't seem worried."

Walking over to where she was standing, he calmly brushed a stray lock of hair behind her ear. "Tink, here are the facts; that night, Pan, Tao and Nate claimed you as their own. It was getting close to your birthday and the three of you agreed that this was the best solution. If Zane says anything different then he would need proof and I don't see how he'll produce proof when there are three very distinct nymph bites on your shoulder and nothing else. Plus, there's a household of people willing to testify that he came into town looking for some trouble that night but not one of them saw him lay a hand on you." He grinned widely, "So why would I be worried?"

Tink suddenly felt as though a weight had lifted off her chest. The way Aron told the story there was nothing to be concerned over and he delivered it so nonchalantly, it was easy to repeat. He was right, she realised, the situation was in capable hands. "You know, I think your calm assurance that everything will be hunky-dory is beginning to rub off on me," she smiled.

"Great! Well, now that's settled, perhaps we could talk about me for a little while?"

Tink grinned at the nymph. The man was positively adorable when he pouted. "I'm sorry. I know the very real threat to my life and the future of the MC being at stake is really inconvenient," Tink said glibly, tongue in cheek.

Aron nodded his head, "Indeed it is. This isn't the Tink show, you know. I need time and love and affection too."

Tink drew Aron into her arms, patting him on the head, "There, there. I'm sorry I've been neglecting you. Tell Aunty Tink all about it. Is it a girl problem?"

"Nope."

"Guy problem?"

"Nope."

"Is it a non-binary gender identity problem?"

"Wrong again."

Tink threw her hands in the air, "You're going to have to help me out with this one. What's up?" Aron rolled his eyes but Tink could tell the gesture was directed at himself rather than at her.

"There is no girl or guy problem ... that's just it."

"I don't follow," she frowned. "Are you saying that because you don't have a girl/guy problem ... that's a problem? See, it doesn't even make more sense when I say it out loud."

"That's because it's dumb," Aron muttered. "It's just that seeing you, Pan and Nate and Tao together and then watching how Caden is with Jon, it kind of makes me want to try it sometime – a relationship, I mean."

"I wouldn't really call what I have going on a relationship," she put the word in exaggerated air quotes. "And I thought you loved having a new conquest each night? For a while there, you and Luca had a tally." *But that was before Luca started spending more and more time with Wendy,* Tink realised. Whilst Luca and Wendy were by no means in a monogamous relationship, things had certainly changed and more often than not her best friend could be caught doing the walk of shame in the wee hours of the morning. Tink nodded, finally understanding. "Well, maybe you should try it. Get back on the horse ... and try riding the same horse, *or horses,* more than once."

"Do you really think I could manage it?"

There was a genuine question in Aron's voice and Tink answered him truthfully; "I don't know. If I hadn't witnessed what developed between Jon and Caden with my own eyes, I probably would never have believed it, but they work together. All you can do is give it a try." With his usually grinning lips pursed into a tight line, he nodded, but Tink could tell he still had a lot on his mind. "Talk about this becoming the Aron show," she joked. Then, coming up with an idea, she asked, "Now, are you going to help me strip Luca's bike down or not? Seems he's been getting a little too lucky lately, so maybe we should give him some work to do?"

"Take it to pieces?" Aron's brows winged up. "Could we hide the transmission?"

"We can do whatever you want."

"Count me in," he grinned.

CHAPTER SEVENTEEN

"So, let me get this straight?" Nate brought drinks back to their table and sat down. "Aron wants a girlfriend? Not a hook-up but an actual girlfriend?"

"Or boyfriend. He's seen how everyone is getting so loved up lately and he wants to try it out." Tink accepted her cocktail with a superior smile. "You guys are rubbing off on him."

"So what is this, like a scouting trip? Are we supposed to be prowling the room for relationship potential and taking down phone numbers?" Nate took a sip of his water and roved his eyes around the ground floor of Club Darling, ostensibly on patrol for Aron but also hoping to catch a glimpse of either Pan or Tao who were working till midnight. His two male lovers had looked especially sexy leaving the house tonight and he was looking forward to hooking up with them sometime during the evening and perhaps putting their private room to use. *And maybe Tink would like to see it too?*

"Think of it more as reconnaissance. And don't you ever tell

Aron that we did this – he'd be mortified," Tink warned sternly.

Nate made a show of zipping his lips sealed because there was no way he would ever mention this to his hulking brother and risk embarrassing them both. The truth of the matter was that he was surprised by Aron's admission; he'd always thought the big guy was not just happy but basking in his flirtatious lifestyle and it was difficult to imagine him with a constant partner. Then again, Nate could fully understand where he was coming from; his own life was much richer since he, Pan and Tao became exclusive and he wished that degree of happiness for all his friends. Monogamous relationships were certainly not the norm in nymph culture, but for some members within the MC, it seemed to be a formula that worked. *And bless Jon and Caden for showing us it could be done,* he thought. Of course, now that their small group had added Tink to the mix, his happiness was all but exploding out of his chest and the only thing that put a damper on things was the situation with Zane and the Magical Committee. It had been four days since they had received the initial letter but there had been no further follow-up. To say nerves were stretched thin was an understatement. Nate felt like he was holding his breath. It was another reason why some fun in the private room would be well appreciated, he acknowledged, shifting a little uncomfortably.

"Okay, what about her?"

With his mind about to go to a dark place, Nate was thankful his reverie was broken; refocusing on the task at hand, he saw Tink subtly pointing to a woman standing just feet away by the bar. She had long auburn hair which curled naturally at the ends and olive-green eyes to match her jacket. "She's pretty," Nate admitted. "But I was thinking of someone more along the lines of ... that." He chose the most stand-out figure in the room; a fact he knew Aron would appreciate. After all, the guy might want a relationship but that didn't mean he was going to change his spots. Aron liked what he liked and although their tastes in women were very different, Nate considered this doing his friend a solid.

"The one that's heavy on the boobage and wearing five-inch heels? Seriously?" Tink rolled her eyes. "Of course you would pick her."

"Hey," Nate held up two hands in a gesture of surrender, "she's not for me remember? I just happen to know Aron's type."

"And his type has blonde hair and boobs? I thought you didn't judge bed partners based on aesthetics."

"We don't when it comes to feeding on lust and desire. But we're still men, honey, and sometimes bigtime boobs are on the menu. He also has a thing for water sprites if there are any here." Tink appeared sceptical but she looked around anyway. When no water sprites walked by, she turned back to him and wiggled her eyebrows.

"So what do you think about Luca and Wendy then?"

"Um, they're good people ..." Nate hedged, unsure what she wanted him to say about them.

"Well duh! What I meant was, do you think they will ever be exclusive?"

"Luca?!" Nate choked on a sip of water. "I don't think so."

"Really?" Tink sipped her drink thoughtfully. "Because I would never have guessed that you three were only having sex with each other but here we are. It's definitely possible."

"It's possible, but rare," he admitted. "And what about Wendy? What does she want? Maybe she could date Aron?"

"Wendy and Aron?" Now it seemed it was Tink's turn to be surprised.

"Sure. And why don't we toss Lex in the mix too? I've seen the way Lex looks at her sometimes – maybe they could start their own quad?"

"A foursome? Like what we've got?" Tink's scoff made it seem unlikely.

"I guess so. It's not like Luca, Lex, and Aron don't know how to share. And they adore Wendy, she's a beautiful, considerate, and patient woman who understands our needs and lifestyle." He bumped Tink's shoulder with his own. "A little like someone else we all know and admire." The more he thought about it, the more he warmed up to the idea. Although, he left unsaid that what the three of them had found together with Tink wasn't just rare but felt like a one-in-a-million shot. Somehow, he'd lucked out.

Tink took an appreciative sip of her drink, mulling things over some more. "Hmmm, you have raised an interesting point, kind sir. Wendy's working tonight; I'm going to ask her what she thinks."

"Do you two tell each other everything?"

"Of course. Don't you share everything with Tao and Pan?"

Nate nodded. "I do." He kept silent about the fact he wanted no secrets between them and Tink as well, including their true feelings for her – and also what he hoped they'd do tonight.

"What's wrong with your face?" she asked. "When you want to say something you get this big crease between your eyes – you've got it right now. Hikers could get lost in there."

Subconsciously trying to smooth out his features, Nate wondered how to broach the sensitive topic. He wasn't sure Tink would be interested but he'd still like to ask. Maybe, just maybe, she'd agree to join him – *them* – in their room upstairs. The club was a special place to the three of them and not just for fun. It was where they had first decided to come together as more than just friends and he really wanted to share that with her. He was also angling for that one last form of acceptance from her – that one final piece of faith.

"Hey."

Pan arrived just as Nate was about to ask, effectively putting his question on the backburner and he took it as a sign from the universe that now wasn't the right time. He was being greedy – and horny. Tink didn't need to prove anything to them and his itches were getting scratched more than satisfactorily. "Hey," he replied. If Nate had thought Pan looked sexy leaving the house, now that his cuffs were rolled up to his elbows and his hair was perfectly tousled, he looked like sex personified. "How's the shift?"

"Great. Really busy," Pan smiled. "The two cases of artisan

vodka we bought practically flew off the shelf. I've just ordered more."

"Fantastic. Where's Tao?" Nate looked around hoping to spot their fourth lover.

"Just about to take his break. We saw you two here and thought we'd join you for a drink."

Okay, so maybe the universe was actually giving him a giant thumb's up, Nate ventured, silently, every part of him perking up and taking notice again.

"You've got missing hikers again," Tink informed him seriously. "Out with it."

"Are you talking about the line between his eyes?" Pan nodded knowingly. "He really needs to get that under control before it gives him high blood pressure."

"I didn't think nymphs could get high blood pressure?"

"We can't but it's an expression," Pan shrugged. He swung to face Nate, "Now what do you need to get off your chest?"

"Nothing," Nate replied glibly. But of their own volition, his eyes flicked to the staircase.

"Nothing, hmmm?" Reaching across the table, Tink took Nate's palm in her hand and traced the lines there with one tickling finger. "You don't have to say it if you don't want to, but how about you let me guess? Or better still, I could tell your fortune?"

***

With Nate's hand in hers, Tink admired the map of intersecting lines and then imagined those same hands all over her body. She had a sneaking suspicion she knew what Nate wanted to ask and it was cute that he was too shy to just come out with it. She smiled at him, understanding his reticence. Whilst it was true that the private areas of the club had never been a personal favourite of hers there had been a reason for that; she'd always thought her sexy nymph trio took new conquests there on a regular basis. Now she knew better.

Looking seriously into Nates eyes before returning that gaze to his hand, she told him, "I definitely see pleasure in your future … the very near future, in fact." She traced a particularly deep groove with a fingertip. "And this line here tells me that tonight something momentous will happen; the signs very much point to multiple orgasms." Nate gulped and Tink took that as a very positive sign indeed.

"Did someone say multiple orgasms? Seems I arrived at exactly the right time then."

Tink grinned as Tao joined their little group, a dishcloth slung unceremoniously over one shoulder. "Pan and I can leave right now if you want to go home," Tao winked. "We have no sense of responsibility like that. Really!"

Tink arched an eyebrow and asked coyly, "Why do we have to leave? This is a sex club, isn't it?"

The three nymphs exchanged looks and shifted uncomfortably. Tink suppressed a giggle. Could they be any more adorable? Although she never partook in the possible pleasures of Club Darling before now, it was definitely something she wanted to do tonight. Since earning her promise that she wouldn't run, they hadn't spoken about the looming trial with the Committee but it hung like a black cloud over their heads all the same. Yes, she was reassured by Aron's casual confidence a few days before and she had no doubt her tribe of Lost Boys would lie willingly and convincingly for her. But the Committee were not easily fooled and it had the most unique and powerful magical creatures at its core. And although Zane was a sick, perverted, sadistic piece of shit, he had one thing on his side they did not; the law. In a matter of months, when she reached her thirty-second birthday, she would have been the legal property of the satyr anyway. The man simply had no patience and had acted prematurely. But what Pan, Nate, and Tao had done had bought her some time and she didn't want to waste a minute of it.

There had been no more talk of matters of the heart and Tink had been able to keep her own fickle heart in check by warding off all intimacy and keeping her fluffy emotions to herself and well away from the consort-bond they shared rather strongly. Yes, they had sex on a daily basis but all other forms of affection were a no-go. She always made a point to untangle herself from the nest of sweaty limbs every night and make her way back to her own room. Sleeping with the three men wrapped protectively around her, waking with her head on their chests and hearing their heartbeats, would make it impossible for her to hide her true feelings. And it wasn't fair of her to burden them with that. They were good men and true friends. If they knew she was in love with them, they would feel the need to placate her and say it back. Hearing hollow words of love from Pan, Nate and Tao would do what Zane could never have the power to do; break her.

Realising she was successfully holding a pity party of one inside her head, Tink shook the thoughts free and pasted a come-hither look on her face. "Well, what do you say boys? Want to show me what makes this place a sex club?"

Nate immediately raised his hand in the air, "Dibs! I call dibs!"

He yanked her body close to his and Tink was gratified to feel the strength of his arousal already. She may never hold their hearts in her hands but she had no doubts as to her ability to hold their dicks.

Pan scowled at his lieutenant, "You can't call dibs on Tink."

Nate ran a possessive hand from Tink's shoulder to her butt, before giving it a squeeze. "Sure I can. I just did. But maybe I should clarify. I call dibs … on Tink's pussy. Tink plus pussy equals mine."

Tink choked on a laugh and watched as Pan's and Tao's eyes very nearly fell out of their sockets. Nate was a warm, steady presence, full of light and laughter and he was rarely blunt or crass - even in his sexual endeavours. The man had moves that could make her scream but he was always respectful and patient. Tink was positive Nate had never said the word *pussy* in his entire life, despite the fact he was a magical being who fed off sexual energy. Tao on the other hand, Tink could well imagine him using that particular word. In fact, Tink now had personal experience with Tao's creative dirty talk. Yet, he was now standing in front of her blushing. Tao, the male nymph, was blushing.

"Gods, Nate!" Tao hissed.

Nate shrugged, "What? You call dibs on my arse all the time."

"He has a point," Pan pointed out, grinning like a mad man.

For some reason, the truth of that statement made Tao's face flush even redder, causing Nate and Pan to laugh and begin teasing the usually stoic, cranky man. Tink sighed, snuggling into Nate's side, content to watch and listen. It was moments like these when she truly appreciated the beauty of her friends, both inside and out. Was it any wonder she was pathetically in love with the trio?

"Tink?"

"Huh?" She must have been standing there stupidly with little hearts in her eyes for some time because the look on Pan's face said it wasn't the first time he had called her name.

"I asked if you were okay with this?" Pan repeated, clearly referring to their plans of sexy times in the club.

Tink ran her palms over Nate's impressive pecs, before leaning up and kissing him hungrily. "I'm more than okay with it. Wasn't I just the one who predicted multiple orgasms?" With that she began pulling Nate in the direction of the darkened left corner – and the stairs leading *down*.

Nate stalled whilst Pan and Tao continued to be rooted to the spot. She arched an eyebrow, "Problem?"

Tao pointed up to the first floor, "Our private room is that way."

"*One* of your private rooms. Correct?" Tink asked. All three men gulped, nodding their heads silently. "I want to see your *other* private room."

"Tink," Pan's voice was shaky, "You never go down to the basement level. You hate it down there."

"I don't hate it. I've just never trusted anyone enough to feel comfortable down there. I've never wanted anyone enough to want to go there. But I trust all of you enough. I *want* all of you enough." And it was true, Tink thought. The lower level of the club had always held little appeal to her – but never distaste. She didn't judge the supernatural creatures or the humans who frequented the basement, it just hadn't been her thing for the reasons she had just confessed. And she wanted them to know that. This club had been their creation so they could live happy, healthy lives in the human realm and Tink wanted them to know she supported them one hundred percent.

Holding out her hands to Tao and Pan, she gestured them over. "I'm so proud of everything you've accomplished here," she smiled and hoped they could see the truth of her words. "Show me."

CHAPTER EIGHTEEN

Convinced Tink was really a siren and not a fairy, Tao followed her almost blindly as she weaved her way through the crowded lower level of Club Darling. Surely only a siren could capture his heart and mind so completely that he would follow wherever she led? Looking behind him, he saw that Pan and Nate were likewise enthralled, gazes sparkling and mouths a little slack as they shadowed Tink as if she were the pied piper of sex. Tao's nymph nature had already been well fed simply being at the club for the few hours previously – as well as the marathon love making the four of them had competed in earlier that day. But as he weaved in and out of the mass of writhing, aroused bodies on the darkened dance floor, he felt his inner nymph stand up and take notice. The beat of the music was pure sex and seemed to reach into his pants and yank on his balls. It was designed to, he knew that. The music pumping from the speakers was magically imbued and the vents periodically pumped out pheromones. It was nothing dangerous and nothing that would cause anyone to do things they didn't want to do. It simply amped up feelings and wants that were already present.

Tink was clearly just as affected as everyone else – or perhaps it was because of himself, Nate, and Pan trailing behind her like lovesick puppies? Either way, Tao didn't care, but the proof of her desire was sprinkling from her wings in a dusting of magenta glitter. As soon as the effervescent dust touched the ground, shining gold bricks emerged and Tao and his two companions found themselves literally following a yellow brick road. Tao shook his head in wonder. Tink's effortless magic really was a thing to behold and although he by no means agreed with the Committee or their laws, he could well understand why the fairies needed to be protected. Tink was a true treasure.

Despite Tao's beliefs that Tink had rarely stepped foot on the lower level before, she made her way straight to their private room down one of the long, low-lit hallways without needing direction. "You act like you've been here before," he said.

Tink's smile was enigmatic as she opened the locked door with ease – using no key he could see. "Maybe I pressed my ear to the door a time or two."

Pan looked as shocked as Tao felt from the admission, "You listened? But the rooms are soundproofed!"

Tink snorted, rolling her eyes and tugging each of them inside, "Fairy, remember? I'm kind of made of magic …" Tink's voice trailed off as her eyes took in the room.

Tao quickly looked around, hoping the furnishings and

equipment wouldn't cause Tink to run. The room was decked out much like many of the other specialised rooms in the club. It contained a rack on one wall with an assortment of toys ranging from paddles to whips and vibrators. There were two different padded benches, one with handcuffs permanently attached and one with a strategically placed hole in its centre. More handcuffs were permanently shackled to a velvet covered, padded wall on the right, and a huge bed dominated the space at the rear of the room near the ornate bathroom.

Tink whistled as she walked over to the rack, "Now we're talking," she said as she picked up a leather crop. The sound it made on her hand as she tested its weight made Tao flinch nervously.

"No," Pan stated the one word with finality.

"But –"

"Hell, no," Pan clarified.

Tink pouted but put the crop back. She then reached for a spanking paddle and Nate quickly yanked it out of her hands. "Hey!" Tink frowned at him.

"Not gonna happen," Nate held the paddle up, which meant it was well out of reach of the greedy fairy's hands.

Tink stomped her foot in the most adorable way, "You guys are no fun. What kind of nymphs are you? Won't even let me give you a little spanking," she grumbled. "Your ancestors are probably rolling around in their graves."

Tao snickered and Pan rolled his eyes – though what Tink said was likely very true. The Lost Boys were the last seven male nymphs in existence. Their species had been so reliant and so fuelled by their base instincts for sex, that orgies had been their priority. Not procreation. Thanks to their ancestors thinking with nothing more than their dicks, their race was on the verge of extinction. Pan had recognised their doom when he was but a child and Tao knew he would have made an impressive king – had he so chosen to.

"I'll show you what kind of nymph I am," Nate's voice was guttural as he threw the paddle aside and yanked Tink over his shoulder before striding quickly to the silk-covered bed in the far corner.

The bed was the size of two California Kings and had been specially made to match the one in Pan's room at the house. It was plenty big enough to accommodate all four of them – as Nate seemed motivated to prove. He already had Tink stripped bare and was feasting on the perfection of her pale breasts. Tao stared, a lust-induced fog clouding his mind until Pan spanked him – *hard* – with the leather-bound paddle. Tao spun, eyes narrowing at his leader, who simply grinned and waggled the large paddle at him.

"Get naked, lieutenant."

Tao weighed up his options but decided this was really a win-win situation for him and he stripped in record time, watching as Pan did the same. Sounds of pleasure from the bed had him turning back around, all thoughts of Pan and paddles somehow fleeing his mind. Nate had Tink pulled to the edge of the bed, her legs draped over his forearms and her back flat against the silk, emerald sheets as he entered her in one smooth thrust. Tink's back arched in a graceful movement as her body accepted Nate's as though it was made for him. *And it was,* Tao thought. *She was made for all of us.* He was convinced of that fact and one day soon, one day *very* soon, they were going to convince Tink as well.

Content to watch Nate screw Tink with abandon and fuel his own desires further, he jolted when Pan's hands caressed his flanks before making their way to his cock. Tao groaned, letting his head fall back on Pan's shoulder and trusting him to take his weight. He and Pan were practically the same height but Tao was broader across the chest and more heavily muscled. Pan was leaner and built more like a swimmer. The contrasts in their bodies never failed to mesmerise him – and turn him on. Tao relaxed into Pan, his body taking on a fine sheen as Pan's hand cupped and shaped his length as though learning the shape and feel for the first time. In actuality, Tao couldn't remember how many times he had felt Pan's magical hands on him just like this. But Tao knew it would never get old. Nor would the sight in front of him.

"Could they be any more perfect?" Pan murmured against his shoulder where he was nibbling and sucking up a hickey.

Tao allowed the marking, tilting his head for further access, before replying, "I can think of one way to improve on perfection."

Pan's slightly evil chuckle followed him as he sauntered up behind Nate and Tink, who had slowed their lovemaking in speed though not intensity. Tao wrapped his hands around Nate's waist from behind and touched where the two were joined, adding friction and heat. Tink's and Nate's moans were music to his ears and food to his senses, causing Tao to hump against Nate's back.

"Tao …" Nate gasped, head turning to the side and lips seeking blindly.

Tao obliged, gripping the other man's long hair in an almost brutal grip and kissing him hungrily. Breaking the kiss, Tao leaned his forehead against Nate's as they stared into each other's eyes, panting harshly. "Love you."

Nate's eyes darkened impossibly further, "I love you too."

"Pan, please."

Tink's urgent begging had them whipping their heads back down to the blonde beauty who was writhing in Nate's grasp, urging his hips to move once more even as she made grabby hands at Pan who stood just out of her reach. Pan's smirk was cocky and lust-filled as he gripped his hard dick and fed it between Tink's lips. Those lush, pink lips parted eagerly, the sight of Tink being filled and taken by their two lovers was almost too much to bear, and Tao quickly grabbed the base of his own dick in order to stave off his release. Nate – clearly propelled back into action by the display – began to thrust his hips once again, causing Tink to let out a thin scream of want. Their fairy was a needy little thing and complimented them perfectly. She was truly their centre of gravity in every way and in that moment, Tao knew there was literally nothing he wouldn't do to ensure her safety and happiness until the end of time.

Tao watched the proceedings for another ten seconds before he caved. He licked his lips, watching the bunch and flex of Nate's taut butt muscles directly in front of him. Leaning in close and grabbing the sweet cheeks with his hands, he whispered, "Dibs."

CHAPTER NINETEEN

Tink snuggled into the warmth beneath her, consciousness held at bay by the sense of peace and safety she was enveloped in. Despite small twinges she could feel in her muscles – and in other places – she had never felt better in her entire life. The hot water bottle beneath her moved and Tink frowned in annoyance because she was too comfy and didn't want to move. She was just about to rearrange all that cozy heat when a hairy leg rubbed over hers. Tink snapped instantly, fully awake. A hairy leg? *Shit! I'm still in their bed*, Tink thought, struggling to remain still and keep her breathing even. After their fun in the boys' private chambers, Tink had been essentially fucked stupid and hadn't put up even a token fight when the three sex gods had insisted she sleep with them. She had been so blissed out and exhausted, she had even allowed them to bathe her in their amazing tub before tucking her in between shared sheets. She must have passed out after that because she had just broken her one remaining rule; no sleeping with her consorts.

Holding her breath, Tink opened one eye only to quickly close it again. A pair of green ones were looking directly at her! *Shit!* She quickly turned her head and found dark brown ones watching her in amusement from behind her. *Double shit!* Scrambling onto her hands and knees, Tink nearly brained herself with her own elbow. How she managed to hit herself in the face with her own elbow was beyond her – she wasn't really that flexible – but she found herself on her butt on the ground, holding her aching jaw. "Triple shit," she muttered.

"Triple shit, huh? Well, they say the best things come in threes," Nate's cheery voice came from above.

Tink blinked up from her position of naked and stupid on the hardwood floor only to find three gorgeous faces of masculine perfection staring down at her with various expressions of concern, confusion, and humour. It was the humour that had her narrowing her eyes and she pushed herself up onto her hands and knees once more, gesturing toward the door, "I'm just going to, ah …" she started crab-crawling backward, not wanting to stand up and offer her naked body like a buffet to three morning woods!

"Tink? Why don't you stay?" Pan offered.

"Yeah, Tink. Stay." Tao grinned at her, "You stayed all night after all."

Tink swallowed audibly, the reminder causing adrenaline to surge through her body. She kept crawling backwards, careful not to make any sudden moves and give them the wrong idea. She had no clue what that was, but her brain was misfiring. Finding a small throw pillow, Tink placed it strategically over her nakedness and struggled to her feet.

"Tink, what are you doing? You do realise we've seen you naked before. Right?" Pan tilted his head like a curious puppy.

Tink laughed, the sound rang with a touch of hysteria. "Ha! Right. Of course." Still, she clutched the cushion to her chest and used her free hand to cover her lower half. No point waving a red flag at a bull, after all. Tink could already see the hunger in their eyes and she knew if she placed herself in the middle of all that flesh again, she would be a goner. "I'll leave you to it," Tink practically yelled, making a mad dash for the door and closing it with a bang behind her.

Tink knew she was behaving like a crazy woman but she was pretty sure that heavy weight on her chest and the difficulty she was experiencing getting air into her lungs, meant she was having a panic attack. Leaning with her back against the door, she tried to suck in some much-needed air. What was wrong with her? Sleeping with them in what was essentially their marriage bed? They had promised her that no-one other than the three of them had ever been in that bed. It was clearly special and was reserved for their unique relationship. It was one of the reasons she never stayed. Plus, she knew sleeping with them would be exactly like it was; warm, comfortable, and safe. And filled with so much love she could practically taste it. How the hell was she supposed to sleep on her own ever again? She was ruined now. Well and truly ruined and the last tiny piece of herself she had been holding back had just gone up in a puff of smoke.

"They're going to break your heart, Tink," she muttered to herself.

"Or maybe they won't. Maybe, if you're brave and put yourself out there, you might get everything you ever dreamed of."

Tink yelped, her eyes flying open as she struggled to hold the tiny pillow over her lady bits. "Aron?" she squeaked. The nymph in question was in a similarly precarious position with a small handtowel covering his very impressive man bits. Tink looked behind him and realised he was standing on the outside of Wendy's door. "What ....?"

Aron smiled, "I took your advice. Why don't you take mine?"

A series of voices could be heard from behind the door, one distinctly feminine and two more that crazily sounded like Lex and Luca. Had Nate been right about the four of them with his offhanded remark last night? Tink wondered. She swallowed, "Advice?" she managed to stutter out.

Aron winked at her, "Be brave," he repeated, before turning Wendy's doorknob and backing in without knocking.

***

Silence reigned for all of ten seconds before the three of them burst into laughter. Pan's breath wheezed from his throat as he doubled over, holding his sides because they literally hurt from laughing so hard.

"Did you see her face?" Nate asked, his large frame jostling the mattress in shared humour.

"And the way she crawled backward like that? Priceless!" Tao joined in, his shoulders shaking.

Pan wiped tears from his eyes, "I think it's safe to say Tink is ours."

Nate nodded his head, "Ours."

Tao grinned, taking a deep breath before releasing it, "Ours," he concurred. "Do you think she knows it yet?"

"Oh, she knows," Pan snorted. "I have no doubt that's what that little display was all about. She knows she loves us. What's more she knows that we know – and it's freaking her the fuck out."

Pan knew what he said was true. He had felt it. Though the bond between them was nothing like a telepathic connection that some magical beings shared when they mated, it was still deep enough and strong enough that they could feel the other's emotions – when they allowed it. It had certainly come in handy many times during their sexcapades, heightening their pleasure and giving them new insights. Being able to feel the love Nate and Tao had for him was a new and miraculous blessing. One Pan never thought he would know. Nymphs did not take partners or mates like many in their world and no such eternal bonds were created. But thanks to Tink, Pan was now as securely tethered to Nate and Tao just as much as he was to her. All four of them were equal consorts. But Tink had been very careful to keep her shields in place when it came to her feelings for them. At first, Pan was sure the lack of emotion was because Tink didn't feel the same way about them as they did for her. But the last few weeks, he had caught the look in her eye, or the genuine warmth in her touch, and he knew Tink was lying to herself – and to them. When she slept wrapped in their embrace, all her barriers had been down and they had been free to feel Tink's affections for the first time. He now had no doubts she felt more for them than friendship and gratitude, but was it love? Was she *in* love with them, heart and soul, the same way they were with her? Pan had just told his two lieutenants she was but if he were being honest, he wouldn't be confident until he heard the words with his own two ears.

Nate nodded in understanding to Pan's earlier words, "She's freaking out because she doesn't believe we feel the same way."

Pan shot a finger at him, "Exactly."

The three of them looked at each other and sighed in unison. Their beautiful fairy was stubborn as hell, and although she had a knack for reading others clearly and easily, it seemed she was oblivious to what was standing right in front of her. Or rather, the three someone's who were – just as Wendy had said weeks ago. Pan had the feeling his sisterly human had been referring to them, but it sure fit Tink as well. Pan knew their agreement to give Tink time to figure out her thoughts and feelings without the added pressure of their own was the right thing to do. In the time before the claiming, they had wanted to prove that they could be monogamous and remain in a healthy, stable, and committed relationship before they approached her. After the first time making love by the pond when Tink had taken their words to be purely platonic, they had not attempted to say them again. As Pan had just thought, they had all felt their relationship shift, slowly but surely over the past weeks and he had no doubt they had been headed in the right direction. But last night had demonstrated they had already arrived at their destination.

When Tink had led them all without fear into their private chambers on the lower level, walking amidst all the sex and the sin to get there, it had proven in a way words never could have that she accepted them. Tink accepted every part of their natures and she trusted them. Unconditionally. The final nail in that coffin had been to wake only moments before to find a snoring, drooling Tink ranged over Tao's chest. She had stayed all night. She had slept with them. Sure, she had just had a minor freak out about it but Pan was confident she would get over it. And if she tried to hide behind her sarcasm and her wit this time, Pan wouldn't allow it. As if reading his thoughts, Nate said;

"Do you think she'll try to pretend last night never happened?"

Pan looked between his two loves, Tao's dark eyes reflecting the same hesitancy and fear that were in Nate's. Pan gripped each of their hands hard, "We won't let her. She loves us. She's just scared to. But we'll make sure she knows she has nothing to fear. Right?"

Tao squeezed his hand, "Right."

Nate mirrored the move, nodding his head, "Damn right."

Pan's feeling of happiness was fast turning to feelings of

friskiness. Hell, he had two of the sexiest men on the planet naked in his bed, who wouldn't be feeling a little frisky? Just as he was leaning forward to tackle them both to the mattress, the doorbell rang. Pan groaned, "The fuck?" he asked no-one in particular.

Tao huffed, looking decidedly disgruntled as his eyes roved over Pan's naked body. "Who the fuck is that? It's not even nine in the morning. Don't people realise it's time for morning sex – not visitors?"

The doorbell sounded again and Nate pushed himself up, "It doesn't sound like they care. I'll go see who it is."

Pan rose quickly, throwing on a random t-shirt and trackpants. They were a little big on him and he realised they must have been Nate's. That sexy fucker was broader and taller than Pan and it never failed to turn him on. He readjusted himself, willing his hardness to go down but figured he was fighting a losing battle as he watched Nate and Tao share casual caresses as they dressed. Caught staring like a lovesick fool, he rolled his eyes when the two grinned at him like morons. Pan cleared his throat, "I'm coming with you."

Tao grumbled the whole way down the stairs and his disposition certainly didn't improve when he saw who was standing on their front step. Pan felt his own cherry demeanour turn sour and his body tensed, poised for flight or fight.

"Pan, president of The Lost Boys and alleged consort to the fairy, Tinkerbell?" The bigger guy in the dark suit asked, his eyes flicking between the three of them.

Pan pushed down the snarl in his throat, clearing it instead, he replied; "I'm Pan."

"Brent Lane and Shaun Miller," he gestured between himself and the silent man beside him. "We're enforcers from the Magical Committee. We're here to inform you that your trial date has been set for tomorrow at 9am."

"What? Tomorrow?!" Nate gasped.

Pan placed a reassuring hand on Nate's shoulder and a steadying one on Tao's in case he decided to kill the messenger. Pan wouldn't put it past him, he felt a sudden need for violence himself. "Great. Thanks. Noted." He went to slam the door in the faces of the two stooges but a shiny black shoe stopped him.

"We'll also be your guests for the next twenty-four hours," Brent – the big guy informed him.

"Guests? Like fuck you will," Tao growled, crossing his arms over his chest.

Brent growled back – a real growl. His inner wolf obviously feeling challenged by Tao's dominance. It hadn't escaped Pan's notice that the two men in front of him were also alpha werewolves. Brent took a step forward but his partner blocked him with his own body.

"Our orders are three-fold, Pan. Inform you of the trial date, stay with you until then to ensure you don't decide to take a sudden vacation, and also observe your dealings with the fairy in question."

Pan's frown deepened, "Observe?"

Shaun nodded, "We will be called as witnesses after assessing your interactions with the fairy in order to judge the validity of your claim."

"Tink," Nate said so softly that Pan could only just hear him over the roaring in his own ears.

"Excuse me?" Brent huffed.

Nate smiled, though his dark eyes were flinty, "The fairy. Her name is Tink. She's not some subject or tool or magical blood bag. She's not *the* fairy. She is *our* fairy. And if you're going to be staying here, I suggest you get that into your heads and show the proper respect. Or us – her three consorts – will be the least of your concerns. Tink will be. And trust me fellas, you don't want a motorcycle riding, pissed off fairy on your arses."

Nate spun and stalked off down the hall and Pan felt his chest puff with pride. "That's one of my consorts," he nodded in the direction where Nate had disappeared to. "I'm blessed to have two more," he grasped Tao's hand, relaxing a bit when it was squeezed back. "One of them just happens to be a fairy. I don't see what the Committee has to do with it, but I am a man of honour. No one is running. Observe away. We have nothing to hide."

Other than an underlying satyr bite, Pan thought silently. And three little words he was dying to say out loud once more.

CHAPTER TWENTY

Tink held her breath where she was listening at the top of the stairs. The trial had been set and it was in twenty-four hours. She could possibly have one more day of freedom before her whole world was taken away from her. Only one more day where she could look into the eyes of her consorts and be held their arms. She was still mortified over her recent moronic behaviour and had been prepared to spend the rest of, oh, *eternity*, hiding in her room. But the appearance of the two werewolves changed things. *And put things in perspective,* Tink acknowledged.

"Tink."

"Shit!" Tink gasped, hand going to her throat in alarm as she spun around. "Wendy! Don't sneak up on me like that." Tink's heart was beating a mile a minute.

"Sorry," Wendy whispered back as she crept up beside her in order to watch and listen to the proceedings below. "I didn't think it would be so soon."

Tink released a shaky breath, "Me either."

"What are you going to do?" Wendy asked.

Tink thought back over the past few weeks, filled with laughter and joy, warmth and security. And most importantly, love. *Love* ... the word reverberated in her mind, quickly reaching her heart. "I'm going to take Aron's advice," Tink told Wendy, decisively.

Wendy looked confused. "What advice?"

"I'm going to be brave."

Wendy clapped her hands and squealed like a school girl, causing Tink to roll her eyes. But she still dragged her best friend into a hard hug, "Thank you," she whispered.

Wendy kissed her on the cheek and all but pushed Tink down the stairs. Tink laughed, feeling lighter than she had in memory as she skipped down the remaining stairs and past the two boring-looking enforcers. "I'm Tink. The *fairy*," she informed them breezily.

Not stopping to let doubts or nerves get the better of her, she strode purposefully into the living room where Pan, Nate and Tao looked to be in varying degrees of nervous breakdowns.

"Tink ..." Nate breathed, looking distraught. "The Committee –"

Tink interrupted, "I know. I heard. The Committee is convening in twenty-four hours."

The three of them hurried over to her, Pan wrapping her in a strong embrace, "I don't want you to worry. We're going to win this."

Tink smiled, caressing his perfect cheek, "I know. I'm not worried. For the first time in my life, I'm not scared."

Her three consorts looked adorably confused and she couldn't resist pecking them all on the lips. "I have some things to say. I want you to know how much I appreciate everything you've done for me over the years. You didn't have to take me on as your juvenile charge. You didn't have to give me a job or friends." Tink reached out, holding Pan's hand between her own. "You didn't have to give me a family."

Pan tugged his hand free, practically yelling, "Stop! Don't do that!"

Tink was shocked. Here she was being all sweet and pouring out her heart and Pan was yelling at her? "What?"

He thrust a finger in her face, "Don't give us your final speech. You know, the big thank you speech – your last rights. You're not going anywhere and we don't want to hear it," he fumed.

Tink raised her eyebrows, the man thought he was so smart. Looking at Tao and Nate she could tell they were as equally pissed, or scared rather, which for men often resulted in the same thing. "Oh, I think you want to hear this."

Tao snorted, belligerence plain on his face, "Hear you tell us thank you for doing you a favour by claiming you before you ride off into the sunset? Yeah, no thanks."

Tink turned to Nate, "Nate?"

Nate clenched his jaw and simply shook his head in mutinous silence.

Tink sighed, "Fine then. If you don't want to hear how much I admire you all for creating such a wonderful family, how proud I am of you all for developing such successful businesses, how grateful and humbled I am that you would sacrifice your own potential happiness to claim me and save me from a terrible fate ..." Tink walked slowly backward, shrugging easily as if she didn't have a care in the world. "And if you don't want to hear how much I love you all ... how I am deeply, irrevocably in love with you; Pan, Nate, Tao. How much I've loved you for years but was too afraid to say it. And how these past weeks have been the best moments of my life because I was allowed to touch you, laugh with you, share your lives – and your bed. That I've never been happier or felt more blessed than I do when I'm in your arms. And that I never ever want to leave, then, well ..." Tink was almost at the door. She shook her head, "That's fine. I won't tell you then."

And three, two, one ...

Tink gasped when she was enveloped by three sets of nymph arms. She grunted when all four of them landed on the hard floor in a big pile of tangled bodies and then laughed when three mouths began kissing her wherever they could reach.

"Tink, I love you. So much!"

"We adore you, Tink. We have for so long."

"You're so beautiful and wonderful and I love everything about you. Gods, we are so in love with you."

"Tink, our best friend, our sensual lover, you're ours."

"We're yours, Tink. Everything we are. Everything we have.

Yours. All yours."

The words and declarations came hard and fast and even though she knew each of their voices better than her own, Tink couldn't make out who was saying what. Her ears were ringing and her eyes were leaking and her heart felt ready to burst from her chest in happiness. But it didn't matter who said what because they all felt the same way. They loved her. Tink was loved.

"I'm loved," she whispered.

Frantic lips and hands stopped and Tink found herself on her back on the rug on the living room floor, hair a tangled mess, wings trapped beneath her as three male nymphs stared down at her with identical shit-eating grins.

"Yes. You are," Pan confirmed, capturing her lips with his own in a toe-curling kiss. "And so are we," he stated, pulling back.

Tink smiled, searching out each of their beloved gazes, "Oh, you are loved so hard right now."

Nate barked out a laugh, "Only you ..." he shook his head before stealing a kiss of his own.

Tao muscled his way in, taking a kiss as well as her breath and she reached up pulling his shirt over his head – at least she tried to. She was disgruntled to discover her three consorts were pulling her to her feet and righting her clothing instead. "What the hell? Where's my 'I love you' sex?"

Pan's smile was full of affection but he gestured to the other open end of the living room – and the two werewolves currently staring at them. "We have guests," he reminded her.

Tink glared at the two men before turning back to her lovers, "So? Aren't the Men In Black here to witness? I say let them watch."

Pan rolled his eyes, Nate snickered and Tao let out a low whistle. "Damn, girl. One night in the private rooms at Club Darling and you turn all kinky."

Tink smiled smugly, purposely brushing by her guys as she sauntered past. "Nymphs may be born sex addicts, but fairies are born flying their freak flag. Gentlemen," she murmured to the two enforcers and they hastily stepped aside, mouths hanging open.

Annnd three, two, one ... Tink thought. Laughing when she was scooped up and thrown over a broad shoulder before being whisked away.

CHAPTER TWENTY-ONE

Pan entered the Magical Committee courthouse through double-wide marble doors carved to resemble a forest entrance. The scale of the doors hinted at the grandiose nature of the building itself; its towering columns supporting a large domed roof made entirely of glass. Everything was polished to a high sheen and glistened in the morning sun causing him to squint even though he was essentially inside. He was just about to turn left and take the corridor to the room where the hearing was to take place when he remembered he had a dog on his heels and spun around.

"I can take it from here," he nodded to the burly enforcer. "Feel free to stay outside like a good puppy."

"I'm not permitted to let you out of my sight."

Brent ignored the insult just as he had ignored all of Pan's quips over the past twenty-four hours and the fact that he couldn't get a rise out of the guy made Pan like him even less. *He was like a robot*, Pan thought. His expression never changed and he hadn't even seen the guy take a piss. Still, the one thing the Committee's goons did respond to was logic, so he said; "You couldn't let me out of your sight until the day of the trial when your duty was to deliver me to the courthouse." He made a show of looking around, "I'd say that job's done, wouldn't you?" He gave the enforcer such a flinty-eyed stare that the man reluctantly bobbed his head.

"I'll be on the steps out front. Don't go anywhere," he warned.

"Wouldn't dream of it," Pan muttered. This wasn't exactly his favourite place to be and it certainly wasn't his idea of fun at nine in the morning when he'd much rather be at home fucking his consorts senseless. In fact, leaving his lovers' tangle of limbs had been particularly difficult this morning; none of them could predict the outcome of the day's proceedings and Pan couldn't help the feeling that three pieces of him were already missing.

You'll see them in under an hour, he told himself firmly. *There's no need to get all dramatic.* And that much was true; he'd only come ahead to scope out the area. He didn't think Zane and his gang would make any trouble today – especially not if the satyr believed the gavel would fall in his favour – but Pan wasn't taking any chances. Tink's welfare was at stake and he planned to check the courthouse thoroughly before he gave The Lost Boys the okay to arrive. Of course, there was still one enforcer at their home and he was tasked with ensuring Tink, Nate and Tao showed up for trial, but one lone enforcer was no match for his men and should he deem this trial a threat to Tink's safety, all he had to do was make a phone call and they'd take her to ground.

The scenario was a tempting one.

Pan had had lots of correspondence with the Committee over the years – too much, in his opinion, and mostly because as so-called King of the nymphs, it was expected that he would serve as a respected Committee member and represent his kind. *Hard pass on that one.* Pan had shunned their repeated offers just as he had shirked the trappings of his station for most of his life. None of it appealed and not because he baulked at the responsibility but because the system was so flawed, and in his mind, pointless. As acting king, Pan would have been a mere figurehead for his dwindling people and as a Committee member, he would be required to sit in on hearings and uphold archaic laws, most of which he didn't believe in. *Super hard pass!*

Because just being in the building caused him to break out in a sweat, Pan folded his sleeves to his elbows as he walked. *With any luck,* he told himself, *in a few hours this will all be over.* Making a silent vow never to step foot inside the building again, he followed the signs left, nodding his head absently to the deferential bobs and bows from passers-by in the corridor – he also caught the odd murmur as he was recognised and even received a full curtsy from a female elf. The whole thing was fucking annoying. In Neverland, he ran clubs and motorcycle shops and no-one cared about his history. Here however, he was easily identified, try as he might to avoid the kingly title. But, as much as it made him uncomfortable, he shelved his scowl, smiled back politely and tried to look regal; just for today, he thought it might work in their favour for him to act as a king rather than a mechanic, even if the idea of it made him twitchy.

Loosening his collar at the neck, he thought about the only other time he'd been here; although the Committee had been in contact many times over the years, he had only entered through that doorway on one other occasion, fifteen years ago. That was when Tink, who had been essentially betrothed to Zane as a mere child, had finally had enough. Just days after her sixteenth birthday, she had broken bonds with her parents and approached him to be her legal guardian. Although she didn't know it, the switch of guardianship hadn't been a simple one, and Pan recalled how he'd marched here all those years ago, skinny and full of bravado, already half in love with a fairy and ready for a fight. Guardians always had sole say in who their ward's consort should be, and given that Zane's own father was a high-ranking Committee member, Tink's family and the Committee had hastily agreed to Zane's early bid. Then, when Tink approached Pan, things had gotten tricky. He'd never told Tink about that day; the day he'd strode into this courthouse and pulled rank for the first time in his life, but he'd never regretted it either. That was the day Tink became safe for the first time and he would have worn the fucking crown if he'd had to in order to make that happen. The fact that she was only safe until she reached maturity had seemed like a small future problem.

Well, that future was now and that problem was currently biting them in the arse. Reaching the courtroom, Pan halted mid-stride realising he was in the room where he might soon lose everything; lose Tao and Nate, lose Tink to Zane and lose everything he and The Lost Boys had built in Neverland. The thought of it chilled the sheen of perspiration on his brow and he felt a tremor pass through him that had nothing to do with the room's temperature.

"You seem nervous."

Pan spun on his heels to see that a woman with olive skin and dark, springy curls had entered behind him and was standing, watching him like a hawk.

"I'm Arya."

Pan couldn't determine the woman's age and although she was beautiful, her demeanour was cold. He noticed she didn't offer him her hand, nor did she volunteer any further information about herself. Responding in kind, he replied, "Is that supposed to mean something to me?"

Arya raised one perfectly sculpted brow. "Should my name mean something to the King of Nymphs?" She cocked her head to one side. "Probably not. But to the man standing before me at trial today, my name will mean everything."

"I don't follow."

"I'll be acting as the *veritas* on your case. Although you might know of me as a seer."

If she used the colloquial term for his benefit, there was no need. Pan knew well the role of a *vertitas* in proceedings such as these. "You're the fortune-teller," Pan murmured, now face-to-face with the very person he'd hoped to avoid. Most hearings brought to the Magical Committee were resided over by a judge much like a human trial, however, very occasionally, the Committee would bring in a mystic. *And a mystic is the last thing we need,* Pan thought, the last of his warmth fleeing his body.

"A fortune-teller?" She shook her head. "Nothing so crass as all that." Arya speared Pan with an all-knowing look. "My purpose here today is to listen to your testimonies then pluck the true words from the deceptions. After all, this is a case with two sides which means that one side must be a fabrication."

"The way you're looking at me makes me wonder if you've already made up your mind." And if that was the case then they were totally screwed. Then again, after she heard their carefully crafted interpretations of that night, things might get even worse. Pan wondered if maybe he should make that call …

"Oh, don't worry. I never make up my mind until all the evidence has been laid out. You will each get thirty minutes to speak and that will include questioning time. At the end of that period, I shall have enough information to determine which statements presented were falsehoods and I will bestow my ruling."

"And have you ever been wrong?" Pan challenged.

Arya smiled but there was no warmth in it. "There is no wrong or right – there is only the truth." She inclined her head, "I will see you very soon, Pan, King of Nymphs."

But when she turned to walk away, Pan, despite his better judgement, called out, "It must be strange to live in a world where everything is so black and white ..." At his words, he thought he caught a small hitch in her step but moments later she was rounding the corner and gone.

"Triple shit!" Pan repeated Tink's phrase aloud to the empty courtroom. Deciding to make the call to his men, he'd just pulled his phone free when the stoic enforcer whom he'd purposely left outside, entered the room and sat down. Not a word passed between them but the man's beady eyes watched him carefully. Behind him more people began their slow trickle into the courtroom and Pan could only glance skyward and shake his head. It seemed that today really wasn't their day.

CHAPTER TWENTY-TWO

Tink entered the courthouse with a werewolf enforcer at her back and flanked either side by the strong presence of Tao and Nate. Both looked not only handsome in their suits but also formidable, and they wore matching expressions which warned the entire room not to fuck with them. Tink knew the looks were meant for Zane and The Hooks but she still felt the need to jab them simultaneously in the ribs. "Cool it with the angry faces, okay? We want the Magical Committee to like us. Make a good first impression and all that."

"Sorry," Nate murmured gruffly. "I just hate the idea of you being on display, especially with Zane in the room." He eyeballed the area for the hairy satyr. "I don't see him yet."

"Good, because if I so much as get a hint that he's undressing Tink with his eyes, I'm going to jump the witness stand and bang his head like a gavel."

"Um, I hate to break it to you, but I don't think there's going to be a witness stand …" Tink's gaze wandered over the rows of ornate marble bench seating which faced one long front table. Off to the left, she saw what looked like a man-sized box formed by crackling magical energy. "I have a feeling that's where we give our testimony." Nate and Tao both followed her line of sight and Tao swore.

"They can't be serious," Nate grumbled.

"If you gentlemen will come with me …" A slight man with an academic look and thinning hair, addressed Nate and Tao. "I will show you to your seats."

Tao looked from the flickering box of energy to where the man was indicating they proceed; the front row of the gallery seating. He shrugged, "It looks like we don't have to stand in the torture cube, after all."

The man smiled at him with a mild air of superiority. "No, the stall is for the lady."

"For the lady?" The scary box was for her? Tink glanced at Tao and saw that he was about to throw himself at the court clerk and quite possibly strangle the life out of him, so as much as she didn't like the idea of being put into what was essentially a magical cage, she laid a restraining hand on his arm. The look she passed between Nate and Tao told them clearly not to interfere. "It's okay. I'll be okay," she told them, hoping that wasn't a lie. In that moment, over the clerk's shoulder, she caught sight of Pan. She just wanted to hold him – to hold all of them one last time – but before she could even smile a greeting, another man was by her elbow, leading her away.

"Why can't I sit beside the others?" she asked. As if in answer, the second clerk flicked his eyes to her currently unbound wings. *Of course,* she thought. *The cage is designed to control my magic.* Although a little flattered that they obviously deemed her so powerful, Tink wasn't keen on the idea of being locked up like some wild animal and she could only imagine the seething rage her consorts must feel at seeing her treated this way. She had purposely muted the bond because their emotions were simply too overwhelming – as were hers – and she didn't want to add fuel to an already raging fire. If the Committee thought she was dangerous, they obviously hadn't seen Pan, Tao and Nate when they were really mad. As they drew her away, Pan's expression darkened and when they reached the box, she caught a glimpse of her three consorts and saw they were all ready to eat bullets and spit shrapnel. *Nope, definitely not me the Committee needed to worry about.*

Stepping inside her magical cage for the day, Tink took a seat and although there was plenty of room to be comfortable, she kept her legs beneath her and her arms folded neatly in her lap. Her wings were the only appendages anywhere near the magical frame but she made certain they didn't touch the buzzing, spitting energy. Using her own magic, Tink could sense the imbued power around her and although she knew the frame wasn't strong enough to cause her permanent damage should she touch it, the magic was certainly powerful enough to cause significant pain. *And probably lay me out flat on my butt!* It was like a dog collar – an electric dog collar, she realised, keeping her on a leash.

"The proceedings will begin in five minutes," a clerk announced.

Tink scanned the courtroom and as if summoned, Zane chose that moment to enter the room and stroll his way through the crowd of people taking their seats. He stopped and talked to a few; obviously knowing many of the attendees whereas Tink knew none. Or almost none; there, lined up against the back wall were her Lost Boys and Wendy. Each wore a suit, and side by side like that, Tink could easily imagine them as groomsmen for a wedding. Lex had even scrubbed the ever-present grease from his knuckles and just seeing that made her become a little teary. Wendy, obviously attuned to her building distress, gave her a signal to square her shoulders and sit tall – exactly the reminder she needed. *And that was what best friends were for,* she thought.

Sitting straighter and with her head held high, Tink purposely ignored Zane in favour of a much more pleasant view; her three consorts in the front row. She smiled at them and prayed the smile conveyed all the love she felt not only in that moment but for the years she'd left the words unsaid, and when they each smiled back, she felt her heart swell; no matter what happened today, no-one could take away what they had created the previous day. Their love for one another would last a lifetime and not Zane, nor the Committee would ever be able to touch it.

"Please stand for the arrival of the honourable Arya, *Veritas* and presider over this hearing, as well as our venerated Committee members."

Tink stood carefully and watched as a woman swathed in a floor-sweeping sapphirine dress and wearing a golden shoulder sash, led the Committee to the dais where they each took their seats. The *Veritas* named Arya took her esteemed place in the centre and when the courtroom was quiet, she spoke.

"Today we address the case brought to the Committee's notice by Zane of the Satyrs, for the claim that he was unlawfully usurped as the fairy Tinkerbell's consort." She flashed her gaze over the gallery, lingering on the members in question. "This claim is refuted in its entirety by Tinkerbell as well as her three consorts, the nymphs Pan, Nate and Tao. Let it be on record that whilst Pan is King in the land of Nymphs, that fact shall have no bearing on today's proceeding and shall not affect judgement in any way."

Tink noticed that there were a few craning necks at this statement with many in the gallery trying to catch a glimpse of Pan. She also saw that Zane's expression hardened as Nate, Pan and Tao were mentioned by name and that the satyr's hands clenched reflexively as though he were again ready for a fight. She noticed that unlike the members of her MC, Zane hadn't done much to clean up for this occasion; his clothing looked as polluted as ever and his fisted hands were etched with grime. But, although Zane's foul countenance might be off-putting, Tink knew that too would have no bearing on the outcome of the trial. Her wings flitted nervously as she waited for Arya's next words, and having never been involved in court proceedings, was surprised when she heard the *veritas* say;

"I realise that many of you are here today to listen to testimony, however I must inform you that each witness shall be questioned in closed chambers. I will be calling each witness individually to discern the truth of their words but not in a public spectacle. This case could well set precedent and whilst the high-ranking nature of the individuals involved shall in no way alter my decision, it does warrant an element of decorum." She surveyed the gallery, challenging anyone to disapprove of her methods and although there were distinct murmurings and a shuffling of movement, no-one spoke up. "At this time, I should also remind the consorts Pan, Nate and Tao that should they be found guilty in this case the minimum punishment is a public flogging whilst the maximum penalty is death."

Death

Although Tink knew what the possible sentence might be, hearing it aloud was chilling. The word seemed to roll itself over and over in her mind until she was headachy, her chest felt tight and she was nauseated. Despite yesterday's bold claim that she wasn't scared, she felt pretty damn terrified right now. Added to that, the female *veritas* didn't look like a woman who took her position lightly.

"I will first call Zane, the satyr into chambers, followed by the consorts individually, then further witnesses."

Arya's gaze shifted to hers and Tink held it without blinking or looking away.

"Finally, I will interview the fairy Tinkerbell and then resume chambers where I will formalise my ruling." She rose and immediately a clerk walked to where Zane was seated and motioned the satyr to follow him.

As Zane stood, he grinned arrogantly at Tink and wet his lips before trailing the clerk into a side corridor. Tink ground her teeth. She could only imagine his glee at being able to tell his sadistic side of the story and wondered if she'd at least get a chance to wipe that smile off his face before she was officially handed over to him as his property. She promised herself that even if they lost this case today, she would still make Zane regret the day he ever placed a bid on her magic.

She was still thinking up various creative ways to make Zane experience a world of hurt as hour by hour the trial lurched on and one by one Pan, Tao, Nate, The Lost Boys, and the two enforcers were called by name and interviewed behind closed doors. Given her lovers' grim expressions as they each returned, the experience with the *veritas* had not been a positive one. By the time Tink's own name was called, her nerves were frayed and she'd worked herself up into a serious state of mad. *I'll tell my story and convince the veritas that what I say is the truth. Then, Zane can take a long ride off a short cliff!* She also hoped that after falling from the cliff he'd crash into the ocean and get eaten by sharks!

***

"Will the fairy, Tinkerbell please follow me."

Those were the words Tink had been both waiting for and dreading this entire day but she kept Wendy in mind and squared her shoulders as she was released from her cage and led away. This was it; time to make Zane disappear out of their lives forever. Following the squat little clerk, she took the opportunity to stretch her wings and snickered only a little when the slight movement caused the man to wince like she'd tried to slap him. "Don't worry, they're mostly harmless," she smiled down at him.

"I don't believe that for one instant … and my business is the truth."

Tink spun and saw that Arya, the *veritas,* was suddenly behind her even though her chambers were up ahead.

"I too felt the need to stretch my legs," she explained. "But perhaps you should refrain from outstretching your wings whilst you are here today – we wouldn't want anyone to get the wrong idea. After all, those werewolf enforcers can be twitchy." She passed Tink on the right and led the way into her private chambers before indicating a chair. "Won't you sit down?"

"What, no cage this time?" Tink muttered.

"Would you prefer one?" Arya's eyes narrowed and squinted at her darkly, reminding Tink of the sparkling azure colouring of a mermaid's lagoon.

"No." She answered simply. "The chair is absolutely fine."

"Good. Then we can get started." Taking a seat of her own, she motioned for Tink to hold out her hand. "Just a simple touch will assist me to determine the veracity of your statements. Now, if you could please start at the beginning."

"The night I was claimed by Pan, Nate and Tao?" The woman's touch was subtle, her palm just barely making contact with Tink's, almost as though it were hovering there. But Tink found it wasn't the physical contact or Arya's eyes that compelled her to listen and answer; it was her voice. The sound was so melodic that Tink imagined it was like a siren's call and she immediately became lost in it like a sailor at sea in thick fog.

"No, from the very beginning," Arya amended. "Tell me now."

"When Zane came to my parents with his offer," Tink nodded, understanding. "I was twelve …"

CHAPTER TWENTY-THREE

Tink had been returned to her magical cage an hour ago and it was now well into the afternoon. She wasn't sure how she felt about the *veritas's* questioning; although the four of them had agreed to mention her altercation with Zane thus remaining as close to the actual truth as possible, she also knew to keep clear of any allusion to the physical attack and her being bitten and marked by the satyr. Tink had been careful to stick to the plan but whilst she'd kept her story straight and tried her very best to keep her breathing even and her voice steady, she knew by simply gazing into Arya's eyes that it most likely wasn't enough. The very nature of a *veritas* meant that they could perceive even half-truths in the same way that a doctor could look at a wound and tell if it was infected. Locking eyes with Pan, Tao and Nate, she gave them a small smile and sent a flood of love their way, knowing it was possibly the last they would share. *My last moments of happiness.*

"All rise." A booming voice echoed in the large room.

Here we go, she thought. Bracing herself, she watched as

Arya re-entered the room, the indigo fabric of her dress flowing behind her, and resumed her place at the centre of the table. Without preamble, she began;

"I have deliberated in chambers and I am now ready to proclaim my findings," she announced. "You have a strong lineage, Zane ..." She addressed the satyr first and had eyes only for him. Her eyes were hard as stone and difficult to read. "Indeed, your father and mother and his father before, each sat on this Committee at some point and they are well respected. It is a privilege to sit at this table and your family have always treated it as such. Know that I hold them in high esteem."

She nodded to the satyr elders as they sat in the gallery and Tink held her breath. She was certain now that the *veritas* knew everything she'd been hiding. All of it, and given the circumstances, there was no way she would rule in their favour. Arya clearly respected the satyrs and the law, and to uphold the law, Zane would win this ... *and win me*. Tink knew she could deal with that – if she had to be handed over to Zane then so be it, but what would happen to her family would be a worse fate than hers and it took all of her willpower not to call out already and beg for an appeal or leniency.

"And you did, in truth, make first offer for the fairy, Tinkerbell, when she was a youth," she continued.

At these words, Zane smiled smugly from his seat and Tinkerbell had to use every ounce of her unravelling self-control not to set his chair on fire. Dragging her attention away from Zane before the smoke truly began to curl, she focused instead on Arya's words.

"Nevertheless, based on what I see before me, you do not share your family's honour nor do you deserve their reputation as legacy. If this trial were to be influenced by my personal opinion, then know, Zane of the satyrs, that my ruling would not fall in your favour."

Everyone in the gallery swung their heads at the sudden angry growls emitted by Zane and The Hooks but Arya continued with her speech as though there had been no such interruption.

"In principle, I struggle to see the value of your bid for Tinkerbell the fairy even as I acknowledge your offer as just under the law. Your idea, as you conveyed it, of the satyrs being made great once again under your leadership is not a just a fallacy but a concern. The colony of which you dream is far from the glorious empire of your speech, and is instead a dystopia and a breeding ground for monsters. I shudder to think what a fairy's magic might achieve when wielded by such ambitions."

Hardly able to believe what she was hearing, Tink squirmed in her seat. *We could actually win this.* Although not quite ready to pop the champagne, everything Tink was hearing now led her to believe they had a chance. And that was why Arya's next words fell like a lead balloon onto her chest, effectively crushing the air from her lungs in the next instant.

"However, there is no truth in opinion, and as such, opinions have no bearing within this court." She turned to nod deferentially to the Committee on her right and then her left. "I shall now lay out the facts, testifying as to their veracity."

No. Tink found she couldn't speak, couldn't turn her head and could hardly breathe. All she could do was watch and listen.

"Zane of the satyrs, lawfully bid on the fairy, Tinkerbell and that bid was accepted by Tinkerbell's parents, who were at that time her guardians. Four years later, Tinkerbell sought out new guardianship and was accepted as a ward by Pan, King of Nymphs until such time as she was thirty-two years old and reached her magical maturity. Any offers on her person until she came of age could be rightfully vetoed by Pan and were so vetoed during the course of his guardianship. At the age of thirty-two, Tinkerbell would no longer require a guardian but a consort to control her magic as per our law, and at that time she would be marked and claimed."

"I made first bid on the fairy – Tinkerbell was always mine!" Zane stood, snarling beside Diesel. "That was always my magic."

"Hush. Do not speak."

The *veritas's* words were firm but not harsh or loud as she directed them at Zane. Even so they held a power and Tink felt her own urge to be silent and noticed a general quiet fall over the room at large. *Perhaps Arya can do more than just detect deception,* she wondered.

"On the night in question," Arya continued, "the fairy, Tinkerbell, was accosted by Zane and his group, The Hooks, and was made to fear for her safety. Using her magic, she escaped the situation unscathed –"

Unscathed? Tink blinked once. Twice. Certain she had heard the *veritas's* words incorrectly. What was she saying? How could a *veritas* state that she'd escaped unscathed when it was then that Zane had marked her? Across the room, the satyr had also noticed the apparent misstep because despite her call for quiet, he was now roaring from the gallery, his men snapping like crocodiles at the clerks who were trying unsuccessfully to call for calm. Tink must have missed the woman's next few words but she heard what was important;

"And as such I declare the nymphs Pan, Nate and Tao to be truthful and lawful in their claim and state with the force of my authority that they shall henceforth be Tinkerbell's consorts."

"What?" Tink stuttered, still uncomprehending. No longer could she hear Zane yelling or the uproar from his men or from the satyrs in the gallery. She was so shocked and so immersed in the thudding of her heart in her chest that she didn't even notice when the clerk dissolved her magical cage. In fact, she could barely see or hear anything at all until three pairs of arms wrapped around her and she was engulfed in the strength and love of her consorts. "I can't believe it," she muttered into their collective chests. "I don't understand."

"I say we count our blessings," Nate murmured into her hair.

"And never question what just happened here," Tao seconded as he urgently kissed Tink's cheek.

"I may never understand it but I don't care." Pan drew Tink to him and kissed her hard on the lips before eagerly embracing his other two consorts. "And I'll never take it for granted."

Around them the courthouse was clearing but Tink didn't care and amid the affections of her lovers and Jon, Caden, Michael, Aron, Lex, Luca and Wendy each taking their turn to congratulate and hug everyone, it was some time before any of them were ready to leave. After too many wonderful embraces to count and lots of comradely backslaps, Tink finally looked about them. The satyrs were gone, she noted and she hoped Zane and his men were already on the road leaving town, and the rest of the courtroom was empty save for a lone couple standing in the corner. As though sensing Tink's eyes on them, the woman turned and she realised it was Arya. Changed out of her official dress, she wore a plain chiffon robe in the purest white and beside her, Tink was surprised to see a fairy; the man's magnificent emerald wings outstretched and flittering madly as he casually touched Arya on the arm. Tink saw some quiet words pass between them and then the man turned his head with a smile. Before Tink knew what was happening, the duo approached.

Despite the fact that the *veritas* had just ruled in their favour, as Arya approached, three protective bodies placed themselves just fractionally in front of Tink. Pan nodded to the pair. "Honourable *Veritas*," he acknowledged. But although respectful, he maintained a shielding stance.

"Pan," Arya bowed slightly at the waist. "I'd like to introduce you to someone." She nodded to the man by her side and caught

Tink's eye, "And I would especially like Tink to meet him. This is Jasper ... my husband."

"You're his consort." Wide-eyed, Tink held out a hand to the man, smiling delightedly when the shared magic between their gripped palms tickled, raining flecks of fairy dust onto the floor.

"She is indeed," Jasper answered. "And the most beautiful consort in all the known lands."

The man's voice was deep and penetrating and Tink found that she liked him immediately. She knew her expression was still stunned, and she peeked around at The Lost boys only to see similar looks repeated all over their faces as well. "Is that why you —"

"Told the truth?" Arya winked. "Yes. I know firsthand how wonderfully powerful a fairy's magic can be ... as well as what it is like to love one." She laid her hand on Jasper's shoulder and when he returned the gesture with a simple caress of his fingers on her back, she smiled. "I couldn't in good conscious give you to Zane. Very occasionally the greater good is more important than the truth."

"You really believe that." Pan was clearly astonished. "But I thought as a *veritas* you had no choice but to speak and rule truthfully ..."

"There is always a choice, Pan, King of Nymphs. In every act there is freewill and that is the greatest truth in existence." She smiled at the three consorts and singular fairy, "And I believe you four have used your freewill wisely ... as have I." With a gesture to her husband, they turned to go but not before Arya spoke over her shoulder, "But if you ever tell anyone about this, I will pit my fairy against yours," she grinned.

"Noted," Tink smiled. "And thank you. From the bottom of our hearts, thank you."

"No thanks are required. Just try to live well and be happy," she told them. Then, arms linked, Jasper the fairy walked with his consort out of the courtroom, leaving Tink, Wendy and their Lost Boys alone.

"Well, you heard her," Tao announced to the room, "Let's go and get our happy on."

Pan and Nate laughed and the sound was musical. And when she suddenly found herself plucked bodily off the ground and carried out the door, Tink knew that she'd never felt happier in her life.

CHAPTER TWENTY-FOUR

Zane couldn't see clearly due to the rage clouding his vision. Ever since the Magical Committee had banged their crystal gavel and handed down their holier-than-thou-fucking verdict that afternoon, everything was pinpoint. The whole world was a peripheral haze but in its centre was her; Tink. They'd taken her from him and they weren't going to get away with it. The Committee would pay for their treachery and Pan and the rest of them would pay for the lies they'd spun. But, from the moment Arya named Pan and his band of pussy's to be Tink's true consorts, Zane had known what he had to do first, what he probably should have done a long, long time ago. Pan and the others would pay soon enough but right now, if he couldn't have what was rightfully his then no-one else would have her either – he'd make damn sure of that. Tonight, he would show Tink what happened to anyone who defied him.

With that sole purpose in mind, Zane drained the last of his beer and left the bar, stumbling down the two steps leading outside. Weaving on his feet a little, he walked across the near empty lot, still managing to bump heavily into a parked car. Righting himself with a hand on the hood and pushing himself semi-upright, Zane heard swearing coming from behind him; apparently the owner of this piece of shit was one of the three guys he'd passed leaving the bar. Hoping for a fight to grease his wheels, Zane turned unsteadily and flipped them the bird.

"Go home, buddy! And sober up!"

One of them – he couldn't make out which one – swore in his direction. Apparently, the loudmouth also needed to prove he had balls and bellowed; "And keep your filthy hands away from my car!"

Zane spun to face him, flipping the old guy off a second time and yelling, "Go fuck yourself."

Despite the man's cock-show, Zane was disappointed that no-one followed him. He was in bad temper and it obviously showed; if anyone started trouble with him tonight, he'd make damn sure he ended it. Thinking that trouble was a sure-fire way to whet his appetite for what he was about to do, he gave the driver's side wheel of the shitbox car a solid kick with his boot before trudging over to his bike, and although he heard angry mumbling coming from the door of the bar, he was left well enough alone.

Bunch of gutless fucks, the thought to himself.

This was the second bar he'd stopped at after the hearing; the first was clearly in cahoots with The Lost Boys because they knew who he was and had refused to serve him. Well, he could blame Tink for that too. Although he'd left without trouble he planned to go back later tonight. Grinning in the dark, he promised himself that after he'd finished with the fairy, he'd burn the bar to the ground. Zane touched the switchblade in his back pocket, reassuring himself that it was still there. He'd taken it from Jagger when the gavel fell, then left the court before any of his men could follow. He didn't need those sorry sonsofbitches messing things up this time. In his mind, it was their fault Tink had gotten away the night he bit her and now they could damned well fend for themselves for a while and learn to really respect his leadership. Without him they'd just be rudderless garbage and when he was gone they might finally appreciate everything he'd done for them over the years. They'd learn to sharpen up. Then, once he'd killed the fairy and righted his honour, they could come crawling back to him. Zane scrubbed his jaw realising that he'd need to think up some suitable punishment for the three of them – then again that would be the fun part.

Locating his motorcycle in the darkened corner of the lot, Zane eyeballed the men on the bar's porch derisively before kicking his bike's stand free of the gravel. He snickered, thinking once more about how none of them were game enough to come after him. *Spineless dogs, all of them. Just like the fucking Committee who listened to the nymph's lies and gave them what actually belonged to me!* Well, they were all going to be taught a lesson tonight.

As he watched, the patrons on the porch lumbered back inside, either too scared or too complacent to pick a real fight. He wasn't too surprised, after all, he'd chosen the foulest drinking hole in Neverland where the clientele matched the taste of the beer; stale and rotting. After he was kicked out of town and refused entry at the other bar, he'd picked a spot on the edge of Neverland, past the warehouses and brothels and where only the most decrepit alcoholics came for their fix. From the outside, the building looked like a ramshackle old shed but inside it was worse. The place was like death's fucking waiting room and it smelt of warm beer and piss. Still, it had served its purpose and while he'd gotten some drinks in him he'd also solidified his plan. Now it was time to put it into action.

Stradling his motorcycle, Zane revved the engine, immediately gratified by the growl of its power. Kicking the bike into gear, he rode a tight circle in the parking lot, purposely spitting gravel, then really opened it up for the road. With tunnel vision, he kept his eyes on the tar as the road snaked its way toward his target.

Tonight, Tink was going to get what she'd deserved all along.

***

Stepping free from the steam of the shower, Tink grabbed a fluffy pink towel from the rack on the wall and wrapped it around herself. Plucking a second for her hair, she tried her best to wring most of the water out before tipping her head forward and securing her white-blonde locks in a skilful twist of the cotton fabric.

Standing and breathing deeply, Tink took a moment to fully appreciate the little things. The last few weeks, although wonderfully momentous, had been hard and even the simplest tasks like taking a shower had been difficult to enjoy – though her three consorts had certainly tried their hardest to relieve her stress in the most pleasurable ways possible. Now, she purposely relaxed tense shoulders and wiped a hand over the foggy mirror to smile at her reflection. Finally, she could be happy. Finally she was at peace.

Grabbing some prettily scented lotion, she squeezed a small amount into her hand and began rubbing it into her body, imagining how the guys would revel in the smell of coconut on her skin. Most of the household were out just now either getting dinner or checking on business at Club Darling and Marooned – both businesses as well as Neverland Motorcycles, had been only rudimentally attended to over the past few weeks and there was a bit of catching up to do. And with multiple witnesses who saw The Hooks leave town, there was finally time to relax. Now, with her body all lotioned-up courtesy of Wendy's stash of cosmetic creams, Tink decided she would allow herself a glass of wine before dinner and when her sexy consorts returned home, they would all eat together … then she planned to offer herself up as dessert.

Dragging the towel from her head and reaching in the drawer for the hairdryer, her mind was so full of the night's exciting possibilities that she almost missed the tell-tale click of her bedroom window closing. Almost. Her wings reacted before her legs did, batting the air and gusting the bathroom door closed. It would have shut and then locked had a boot not lodged itself between the door and the jamb.

"Where's my fairy?" the husky voice grunted. "I know she's in there."

Zane pushed the door wide with a meaty hand and the sight of him stole the scream from Tink's lungs. For an instant he just stood ogling her; a slack-jawed look of drunken desire contorting his ugly features into something even more sinister.

"I've got a real hankering for you," he whispered.

Zane's bleary eyes were fixated on her breasts, clearly imagining what was beneath the towel, but his preoccupation provided her enough time to find her voice. She didn't use it to scream again. "I warned you not to come back here, Zane. You've lost and there's nothing you can do about it."

The satyr flashed her a grim smile and reached a hand into his back pocket. "Oh, I think you're wrong about that. There's definitely one thing I can do. I'm going to cut off your wings and cut out that sharp tongue of yours." Pulling the switchblade free and opening it with a flick of his wrist, he pointed it at her. "Bet you weren't expecting this?"

The sight of the knife didn't faze her, especially not now that her magic was so well controlled. "I wasn't expecting it but I should have been," she admitted more to herself than to him, letting his threats roll over her. Zane didn't scare her – he was nothing. Inconsequential. Still, she should have known The Hooks were too dull-witted to realise when they were beat. With one hand fisting the towel at her chest so that it didn't slip, she shook her head at him, "You always were a blunt instrument, Zane. You never learn." Then she looked past him. "Where's your gang?"

"Just me this time," he swaggered two proud steps into the room with her. "It's just us."

"So no-one to back you up," Tink tsked and shrugged a shoulder, "Your funeral."

Zane must have sensed that she was about to act because in that moment he lunged at her and although his steps were lumbering, his ample weight propelled him forward. Tink had a fraction of a second to bring her power to life and the room shook at the exact same time as his blade bit into her skin. The sting of the knife was secondary to the worry that it might strike again and as the mirror crashed at her back and the plaster cracked, she made the earth rumble again causing Zane to lunge totteringly to one side and clutch at the door frame in order to remain standing.

"Fairy bitch!" he grunted. He thrust his knife at her again but the shuddering ground made it go wide.

Tink spared a singular glance for her burning injury – a small puncture wound just below her clavicle before calling upon more of her magic. As Zane hissed and snapped profanities at her, the house continued to shake and her power encircled his neck like a rope, tightening each time he struggled.

"I tried to warn you," she whispered.

"Tink!"

It took a moment for her to realise that the background noise she'd been hearing wasn't the pounding blood in her ears but fists thundering against her bedroom door. Of course her three consorts would have been able to feel her use of magic. They were the ones grounding it at the source now, after all. They hadn't yet explored what the consort bond could do as far as her magic went, but it was definitely something on the agenda. Pan, Nate and Tao had already argued with her about that. They wanted nothing to do with her magic – they simply wanted her. But sharing her magic with her lovers was something she wanted to do, and because the three nymphs were suckers, Tink knew she would win the argument.

One more loud bang preceded the door crashing inward, wood splinters flying as half the household tumbled into the room. Pan was in the lead flanked either side by Nate and Tao but at the sight of her, shock pulled them up short. "You're bleeding!" Pan gasped, and he would have rushed at her then had Tink not held up a restraining hand.

"Stay there," she said.

Tao's eyes were cautiously wary and he barely spared a look for Zane who was now writhing and choking on his back, and instead locked eyes with her. "Sweetheart, you're hurt. Let us help you."

Tink glanced down to where her blood was soaking the towel. She was by no means mortally wounded but the injury still hurt like a bitch. Still, there was something she needed to take care of right now because if she didn't, she was afraid she'd never be free. Tugging on her magic, she tightened the cord around Zane's neck, watching dispassionately as his face turned an interesting shade of purple. "I think this is as pretty as you've ever looked, Zane. Asphyxiation suits you."

Zane gulped a reply, his hands tugging fretfully at the rope as panic truly set in.

"Tink …" Nate implored. "You're not a killer. You don't really want to do this. Let us help you." He reached out a beseeching arm.

Tink shook her head. "Actually, I really, really do want to do this. I've wanted to do it for a long time." In that moment, Tink unleashed her powers, feeling the ecstatic tremor of magic course through her and knowing it rattled the teeth of everyone in the room. Then, suddenly it erupted; a sparkling rainbow of colours which obscured everything and everyone like a dust storm. As the powder settled, raised voices called out and strong arms engulfed her.

"Sweetheart," Pan scooped her up in his arms, heedless of the blood as it soaked his shirt. "Are you? What? Do you –"

"Pan, I'm okay." Still on a magical high, she giggled, "Although my shoulder hurts – getting stabbed really isn't much fun." There were more arms ensconcing her then, carrying her to the bed where many more hands and worried expressions were waiting.

"How did we let this happen?!" This was from Wendy. "I knew I shouldn't have left you alone!"

"I'm fine, Wendy. Pinky swear." She held out her pinky finger for her friend to squeeze, something they'd been doing for years.

"You're far from fine," Tao snapped, his usually strong voice quaking a little. "Pan, apply more pressure to that wound, I need to go get the medical kit."

"You're all overreacting," she told them but there was no harshness in her voice. They were all here, she realised. Everyone was now here together and they were all safe. They'd always be safe now. She peered over Nate's shoulder at the spot where Zane once laid and sighed out her relief; he certainly wasn't going to be able to hurt anyone ever again.

Whether it was because of their shared bond or because they caught Tink's look, Pan kept pressure on Tink's wound but glanced back to where Zane had had the life choked out of him by Tink's magic. Or, at least they thought he had. "Ummm ... is that a baby goat?" he asked quietly.

"Well ..." Tink began.

"That's Zane!" Nate's eyes practically popped out of his skull as he clearly recognised the man's salt and pepper beard hairs on the goat's chin.

"But it's so ..."

"Cute?" Tink finished Wendy's sentence. "Yeah, I couldn't help myself. Who's ever seen an ugly baby animal anyway?"

"Okay, I have the medical kit –" Re-entering the room, Tao balked at the sight before him. A tiny, prancing, brown and white billy goat. "But ... I thought ..."

"You thought I'd killed him?" Tink shook her head. "Not really my style, although I was a tad tempted. Then I thought of all the magical possibilities and decided that this would be one Zane would hate the most; a cruel satyr reduced to an adorable baby animal."

Pan looked down at goat-Zane and snickered. "You know, if you stare really hard into his tiny goat eyes, he does look pretty annoyed."

"If you think he's prickly now just wait until we donate him to the petting zoo. Imagine those cute kids with their ice-cream-sticky fingers patting him on the head all day long!" Tink laughed as she smirked.

"For Zane, that truly is a fate worse than death," Nate grinned. Taking Tink by the chin, he looked into her eyes then kissed her long and deep.

Because the kiss managed to curl her toes, her shoulder was easily forgotten. As he pulled back ever so gently, she asked, "What was that for?"

"Because I'm proud of you, and because we almost lost you tonight. I never want to almost lose you again, Tink."

"I second that! Move over!"

Despite his gruff words, Tink noticed Tao gently brushed Nate's back as he moved in to claim her for himself. Then, there was only sensation as Tao's lips kissed their way up her neck and plundered her mouth. He kissed her hotly then he took that same heat to Pan's lips right before their leader moved over to her in turn, in order to gently lay kisses on her cheeks, her eyes and finally her lips. *Holy hell!* Now that her body was filled with happy sex hormones, Tink wanted more from them than mere kisses but given their audience as well as her condition she understood that might have to wait.

Still, as Pan eased back, his eyes slightly glazed over, she gripped his hand. "I think this might be the happiest I've ever been," she admitted honestly. "I'm so lucky to have you all." And with those words she roved her gaze around the room. These were her lovers, her Lost Boys and her best friends and she never intended to let them go. Any of them.

"We're the lucky ones," Nate, Tao and Pan announced in unison.

"We love you so much, Tink," Pan told her. "And we're going to use our entire lifetimes to prove it to you."

"I love you too." At her words, Zane-goat gave an annoyed bleat and kicked his back legs crankily. "I think Zane wants to say something," she laughed.

"Too bad we don't speak goat," Nate grinned at the little guy just to annoy him.

"How long will he stay like this?" Tao asked.

Tink shrugged. "Forever, or until I think he's learnt his lesson – whichever comes first. But Zane always was a slow learner."

Tink felt her smile widen, "So I think he might be this way for a long, looong time." She reached out, clinging to the hands of her consorts, "And do you know what else is going to last a long, looong time?"

Pan's blue eyes softened as he raised free hand to cup her face tenderly, "Our love for each other?" He offered, romantically.

Tink shook her head, winking cheekily, "Multiple orgasms!"

Everyone in the room bust into laughter. "Only you," Nate said, shaking his head, but he said it with a smile.

Yes, only me, Tink thought, silently. *Only I could be so lucky.* But casting a quick look to where Wendy was huddled between Lex, Luca, and Aron, and also to Jon snuggled in Caden's embrace, she couldn't help but wonder if The Lost Boys were perhaps a fairy tale and that Neverland was a true place of magic where dreams came true. Whatever the reason, Tink didn't really care. All she cared about was that they were all going to live happily ever after.

THE END

OTHER TITLES BY MONTANA ASH

The Elemental Paladins Series (paranormal/urban fantasy romance)
WARDEN
PALADIN
CHADE
RANGER
CUSTODIAN
REVOLUTION

The Forbidden Series (paranormal, mystery reverse harem/polyamorous romance)
FORBIDDEN HYBRID

The Familiars Series (paranormal reverse harem/polyamorous romance)
IVORY'S FAMILIARS

FOLLOW MONTANA

Email: montanaash.author@yahoo.com
Website: www.montanaash.com
Facebook: www.facebook.com/montana.ash.author
Twitter: twitter.com/ReadMontanaAsh
Montana's Maniacs: www.facebook.com/groups/montanasmaniacs

OTHER TITLES BY T.J. SPADE

The Forbidden Series (paranormal, mystery reverse harem/polyamorous romance)
FORBIDDEN HYBRID

The Everett Files (crime fiction/thriller/romantic suspense)
TAKE YOU APART
TAKE YOU TO HELL
TAKE YOU HOME

Tucker PI (romantic suspense)
SWEET DREAMS: A TUCKER PI NOVEL
SKULL ISLAND: A TUCKER PI NOVEL

FOLLOW T.J.

Email: tjspade@hotmail.com
Website: tjspade.weebly.com
Facebook: www.facebook.com/tjspade
Twitter: twitter.com/TJSpadeauthor
Team Spade: www.facebook.com/groups/498286397010964

Printed in Poland
by Amazon Fulfillment
Poland Sp. z o.o., Wrocław